[美]玛丽

34

SEASON OF THE SANDSTORMS

可怕的沙尘暴

主译:蓝葆春　蓝纯
翻译:李倩

湖北长江出版集团
湖北少年儿童出版社

★ 名人推荐 ★

陈乃芳：美国麻省大学高级访问学者，曾任驻比利时使馆兼驻欧盟使团教育处参赞，北京外国语大学校长；第九、十届全国政协委员，政协外事委员会委员，中国高等教育学会高教管理研究会副理事长，中国教育国际交流协会常务理事，《国际论坛》杂志主编；由泰国王储授予名誉教育学博士、由英国兰卡斯特大学校长亚历山大公主授予名誉法学博士，并有多部论著。

亲爱的少年读者们：

你们好！最近我有机会阅读了一套英汉双语版的系列丛书，名字叫做《神奇树屋》(Magic Tree House)，作者是当今美国最著名的少儿读物作家之一——玛丽·波·奥斯本。几乎全美国的少年儿童都喜欢读她写的《神奇树屋》，把她当作自己的好朋友。我虽早已年过六旬，但是我和美国的小朋友们一样，一拿到这套书就爱不释手，不到两天就全部读完了。

你们也许要问：您为什么这么喜欢这套书呢？

我的回答是：首先，作者的创作思路紧紧扣住了小读者渴求知识、喜欢冒险、充满好奇和富于幻想的心理特点，成功地打造了神奇树屋这个平台。神奇树屋挂在森林里最高的一棵橡树的顶上，里面堆满了图书。它的神奇之处在于小读者翻开其中的任何一本书，指着书中的一幅插图许愿说"我希望到那里去"，梦想就能即刻实现。其次，作者充分发挥"魔法"的作用，轻松自如地引领读者穿越时空，周游世界。从见识白垩纪恐龙时的翼龙和冰河时代最凶猛的野兽剑齿虎，到体察今日的澳洲袋鼠；从了解美国早期荒凉西部的牛仔生活，到欣赏古代中国牛郎织女的传奇故事；从游览古埃及的金字塔到身陷2000多年前中国的秦始皇陵；从遭遇加勒比海的海盗到幸会东方的日本忍者；从历险维苏威火山的爆发到探秘亚马孙河的热带雨林……真是随心所欲，神游八方。再者，作者成功地塑造了杰克和安妮这一对小兄妹，通过他俩的所见、所闻、所思、所想和亲身历险，把历史故事、神话传说、科普知识、人文传统等栩栩如生地展现在读者面前，让你如同身临其境。最后，这套书不仅内容丰富有趣，而且文字浅显易懂，让人捧读之下，不忍释手。

　　为了把这套优秀的少儿读物介绍给全中国的中小学生，湖北少儿出版社特别邀请了我的老同学、老同事、老朋友蓝葆春爷爷和他的女儿——北京外国语大学的蓝纯教授负责全套丛书的汉语翻译。他们的译文既忠实于原文，又琅琅上口。所以我建议小读者们在阅读过程中先读译文，再读原文，这样一书两用，既增长了知识，又提高了英语，算是一举两得吧。

　　最后我想感谢两位译者请我作序，让我有了先睹为快的机会。也感谢湖北少儿出版社为全中国的中小学生们献上的这份大礼。

　　祝你们阅读愉快！

陈乃芳

目录

黄金时代
The Golden Age

"我们到时候自然就明白了！"安妮说，"但是，我们首先要去到那儿才行。快许愿吧！"

"好的。"杰克说。他指着书的封面说："我希望我们可以去巴格达的黄金时代。"

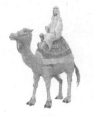

杰克把数学作业扔到一边，打开床边的抽屉，拿出一本手工装订的小书。这已经是他第一百次看这本书的封面了：

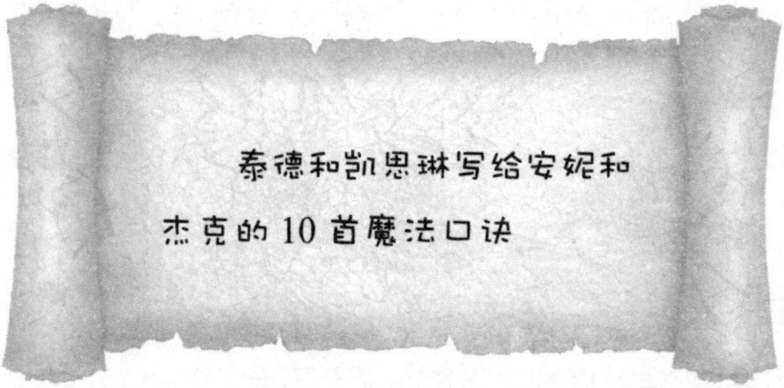

几周以来，杰克一直把魔法书藏在抽屉里，想着他和安妮什么时候才可以再次使用这些魔法。书上的十个魔法口诀可以在四次任务中使用，但是每个口诀只能用一次。杰克和安妮在意大利威尼斯的任务中已经用掉了两个口诀。

“杰克！”安妮冲进杰克的房间。她的眼睛灼灼有神。“带上书！我们走！”

“去哪儿？”杰克问。

“你知道的！快来！”安妮一边喊一边跑下楼。

杰克迅速把泰德和凯思琳的书塞进书包。然后穿上夹克，跟着安妮跑下楼。

安妮正在前面的走廊等他，"快点儿！"她催促杰克。

"等等！你怎么知道它在那儿呢？"杰克问。

"因为我刚刚看见它了！"安妮大声回答。她迅速走下台阶，穿过庭院。

"你看见了？真的看见了吗？"杰克追上安妮，继续追问。这会儿的午后有些寒冷。

"是的！是的！"安妮不耐烦地回答。

"什么时候看见的？"杰克穷追不舍。

"就在刚才！"安妮说。"我正从图书馆往家走，突然有了这种感觉——就去看了看！它果然在那儿等我们呢！"

杰克和安妮向蛙溪湾的树林跑去。他们走在嫩绿的苔藓上，穿过刚刚冒出新芽的树木，来到最高的那棵橡树下。

"看见了吧！"安妮说。

"果然回来了！"杰克惊叹道。他盯着上面的神奇树屋，只见绳梯一直垂到地面的苔藓上。安妮开始往上爬，杰克跟在后面。他们进入树屋后，杰克取下背包。

"瞧，有一本书和一封信！"安妮说。她拿起地上封着的信封，杰克拿起那本有着金色封面的书。

"巴格达。"杰克说。他把书拿给安妮看,书名是:

巴格达的黄金时代

"黄金时代?"安妮说,"听上去不错,我们去吧!"

"等等,咱们先看看信吧!"杰克建议。

"对!"安妮赞同。她打开信说:"是梅林写的!"然后她

念道:

> 亲爱的蛙溪湾的杰克和安妮:
>
> 你们这次的任务是去很久以前的
> 巴格达,帮助哈里发向世界传播智慧。
>
> 要想成功完成任务,你们必须谦
> 逊并且准确地使用魔法。
>
> 遵循——

"等等,哈里发是谁?"杰克打断安妮,"还有,梅林说'向世界传播智慧'是什么意思呀?"

"我也不知道。"安妮说,"我先念完再说吧!"她接着念道:

> 遵循下面的指示:
> 在繁星满天的寒冷夜晚,
> 乘坐沙漠之舟,
> 穿过沙尘和酷热的早晨。
>
> 在屋顶上找到一匹马,
> 它可以看见所有的东西。
> 它在市中心第三堵墙的后面。
>
> 在有树的房间里,
> 鸟儿唱歌的下方,
> 遇见你们的一位老朋友和一位
> 已经认识的新朋友。
>
> 记住,生活中充满了奇迹!
> 在月亮升起之前回到树屋。
>
> ——M

"听上去挺简单的!"安妮说。

"不,不简单!"杰克说,"这些指示都很神秘。我们不知道其中任何一个指示的意思。"

"我们到时候自然就明白了!"安妮说,"但是,我们首先要去到那儿才行。快许愿吧!"

"好的,"杰克说。他指着书的封面说:"我希望我们可以去巴格达的黄金时代。"

风开始刮了起来。

树屋开始旋转。

它越转越快。

然后一切都静止了。

完全静止了。

陌生的地方

Nowhere

　　杰克和安妮用手遮住刺眼的阳光，向窗外望去。他们发现树屋降落在一片棕榈树林中最高的一棵棕榈树上。树下长着浓密的灌木和稀疏的绿草，还有一眼小泉水在冒着水泡。棕榈树林四周是连绵的灼热的沙漠。

杰克觉得很热。他睁开眼睛。炽热的阳光洒进树屋。他和安妮穿着用绳子系住的长袍，头上戴着白色的头巾，脚上穿着尖头的靴子。杰克的背包变成了皮革做的挎包。

"我们看上去像玛莉舅妈送的那本书里的人。"安妮说，"就是那本《阿拉伯的神话故事》。"

"没错儿，就像阿拉丁和阿里巴巴。"杰克说。

杰克和安妮用手遮住刺眼的阳光，向窗外望去。他们发现树屋降落在一片棕榈树林中最高的一棵棕榈树上。树下长着浓密的灌木和稀疏的绿草，还有一眼小泉水在冒着水泡。棕榈树林四周是连绵的灼热的沙漠。

"我看这儿不像是黄金时代。"安妮说。

"是啊，巴格达在哪儿呢？"杰克说。他拿出指导书，翻到第一页，大声念道：

从公元后 762 年到 1258 年，阿拉伯经历了一个黄金时代。

在那个时代，叫做哈里发的统治者管辖着绵延数千里的国家。

阿拉伯帝国的首都是巴格达市，那里是帝国的文化和贸易中心。

杰克抬起头说："这么说，哈里发就是一位统治者了，而且他很可能就住在巴格达。"

"没错儿，但是我们怎么样才能去到那儿呢？"安妮问。

"耐心一点！"杰克说，"记得在上一次任务中，我们学会要按照一定的顺序来做事。"他拿出梅林的指示，又把第一部分读了一遍：

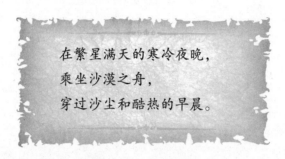

在繁星满天的寒冷夜晚，

乘坐沙漠之舟，

穿过沙尘和酷热的早晨。

"沙漠之舟是什么呢？"杰克思索着。

"不管它是什么，我相信我们最后一定可以找到它的。"安妮慢慢地说，她想要表现得耐心一些。"我们可以先坐在这儿，看是否有大船经过这片沙漠，或者……"

"或者什么？"杰克问。

"或者我们可以试试泰德和凯思琳的魔法口诀。"

"现在还不是用口诀的时候。"杰克说，"梅林说过，我们要准确地使用魔法。我们才刚刚到这儿，不能马上就用口诀。而且，我们在上一次任务中已经用掉两个口诀了。现在我们只剩下八个，要分配给三次任务……"

"好吧，好吧！"安妮打断杰克的话，"只有在实在没有办法的时候我们才能使用魔法，对吗？"

"没错儿！"杰克说。

"那么……"安妮问，"你认为我们现在应该怎么办？"

"我们可以从走路开始。"杰克回答。

"走去哪儿？"安妮继续问，"哪个方向是巴格达？"

杰克望向窗外，只见棕榈树林四周除了沙漠和天空，什么都没有。远处是孤零零的沙丘，整个沙漠安静得有些古怪。

"我们可以……"杰克想不出其他任何事情可以做，"我们可以看看那本魔法书。"他说。杰克从包里拿出魔法口诀书，和安妮一起浏览目录。

"让石头复活！"安妮说，"这个口诀我们在上一次任务中已经用过了，这次不能再用了。"

"反正这个也没用。"杰克说。他开始查找其他的口诀。"把铁变弯！"他读道。"这个我们也用过了。"

"变成鸭子！"安妮说着看向杰克。

"这个不行！"杰克说。

"修理不能修理的东西！"安妮念道。

"没有东西需要修理。"杰克说。

"这个怎么样？"安妮问，"在陌生的地方创造出可以帮忙

的人。"

"嗯……"杰克说,"也许……"

"来吧,这个正合适。"安妮说,"我们现在就是在陌生的地方,而且我们也需要人来帮忙。"

"好吧!"杰克说,"我来念泰德写的那部分,你念凯思琳用海豹语写的那部分。"

"好的!"安妮说。她翻到魔法口诀所在的那一页,然后把书递给杰克。

杰克一字一顿地大声念道:

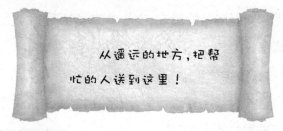

从遥远的地方,把帮忙的人送到这里!

安妮接着念道:

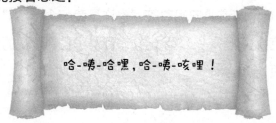

哈-咦-哈嘿,哈-咦-咳哩!

安妮念完口诀的那一刻,沙漠上空突然刮起一阵风,风把沙子吹进树屋,晃动着棕榈树。安妮的眼睛里也吹进一些沙子。"哇!"安妮大叫起来。

"快回来!"杰克大喊道。

杰克和安妮从窗户边跳开。他们靠墙站着,遮住脸。更多的沙子被吹进树屋。

"是沙暴!"杰克说。

灼热的沙子在地板上堆积起来。过了一会儿,风停止了,又恢复到最初的平静。棕榈树也不再晃动。

杰克和安妮向窗外望去,空气中弥漫着厚重的沙尘,什么都看不清楚。但是,沙漠已经恢复了刚才的宁静。

"沙暴应该结束了吧!"安妮说。

"希望如此!"杰克说,"为什么我们的魔法口诀带来的是沙暴而不是帮忙的人呢?"

"我也不知道,"安妮回答,"也许是我们念错了。"

杰克拂掉指导书上的沙子,在目录中找到沙暴的介绍,翻到那一页,念道:

沙漠中的沙暴季节开始于二月中旬，延续整个春天。

风速可达每小时 40 英里。

沙暴很容易让旅行者在沙漠中迷路。

"我不明白！"杰克说。"我们需要的不是迷路，而是找到我们的路呀！"

就在这时，外面传来一阵铃声。

杰克和安妮向窗外望去。透过尘雾，他们看见四个人。那

四个人穿着颜色华丽的长袍,骑在高高的骆驼上,后面还跟着十几只首尾相连的骆驼。骆驼一边走一边左右摇晃,脖子上的铃铛叮咚作响。

安妮笑了。她大声喊道:"帮忙的人来了!"

马姆

Mamoon

"你们现在需要休息！"他说，"愿意和我们一起喝茶吗？"

"当然愿意！"安妮说，"对了，您叫什么名字？"

"我的名字很长。"他笑着说，"你们可以叫我马姆。"

安妮从窗户探出头，"嗨！"她大声叫喊。

"嘘嘘！"杰克把安妮拉回来。"不要让他们看见我们在上面！很难向他们解释神奇树屋的事儿。我们先下去吧！"

"对呀！"安妮说着把梅林的信递给杰克，爬下绳梯。杰克拿起挎包，把梅林的信、指导书和魔法书放进去。他把挎包背在胸前，也爬下绳梯。

来到地面后，杰克把绳梯卷起来藏在树干后面，这样就不会被人发现了。"好了！"他对安妮说。

"嗨！"安妮一边打招呼，一边挥舞着双臂。她和杰克向空旷的地方走去。

骑骆驼的四个人向棕榈树林走过来。领头的人让他的骆驼跪下。当安妮和杰克向他跑去时，他从骆驼上爬下来。他穿着白色的长袍，留着黑色的胡子，长着一双炯炯有神的眼睛。"你们是谁？"他严肃地问，"你们从哪里来？"

"我是安妮，这是我的哥哥杰克。"安妮回答。"我们的家在离这儿很远的蛙溪湾，在宾夕法尼亚。"

"我从来没听说这个地方。"这个人说，"你们是怎么独自来到这个沙漠的？"

"哦……"杰克不知道该怎么回答。

"我们是和家人一起来的。"安妮说。"我们停下来在这里休息,我和我哥哥在树后面睡了一会儿。等我们醒来时,发现

其他人都不见了。他们不小心把我们丢下了。因为我们是一个大家族,有很多的兄弟姐妹——"

"安妮!"杰克打断安妮,因为他觉得安妮说得太多了。

那个人看上去很关心杰克和安妮。"那他们为什么不回来找你们呢?"他说完凝视着沙漠的远方。"我希望他们没有遭到强盗的袭击。"

"这里有强盗吗?"安妮问。

"沙漠里潜伏着很多强盗。"那个人说。

杰克焦急地看着广袤的沙漠。

"这就是为什么一定要和其他人一起出行!"那个人继续

说。"但是我希望你们的家人安好，并且很快就会回来找你们。"

"稍等一下！"安妮很有礼貌地说，"请问你们是谁？你们是怎么突然出现在这里的？"

"我是商人。"那个人解释道。"我们的商队从西边过来的时候，突然遇上了沙暴。这沙暴不知来自何方。但幸运的是，它把我们带到了这片绿洲。我们会在这儿休息一会儿，让骆驼喝点水。等到太阳下山后，我们会趁着凉爽的夜晚去巴格达。"

原来他是商队的头领。他走向另外三个人，对他们说了几句话。那三个人也爬下骆驼，取下包裹。

安妮转向杰克，悄悄地说："瞧，我们的魔法起作用了！这场沙暴就是魔法！它为我们带来了去巴格达的商队！"

"但是怎么样才能让他们帮助我们呢？"杰克问。

"梅林的信里告诉我们要谦逊，那我们先过去帮助他们

吧！"安妮说着就走向那个头领。他正在往一个桶里灌泉水。

"你好！"安妮说，"有什么需要我们帮忙的吗？"

他对安妮笑了笑。"是的，谢谢！"他说，"如果你们能帮忙采集一些椰枣果就太好了。我们的人很饿。"他递给安妮两个大大的篮子。

"没问题！"安妮说，"我们这就去摘椰枣果。"

安妮拿着篮子去找杰克。"你知道什么是椰枣果吗？"她小声，"他让我们去采一些椰枣果。"

"我来查查。"杰克说。他转过身，背对着商队，从包里拿出指导书，找到椰枣果的解释。他读道：

> 椰枣果是沙漠中的一种水果。
> 它们一簇一簇地挂在棕榈树上。
> 人们通过摇晃树干采集椰枣果。
> 椰枣果不仅是一种重要的水果，它的果壳和叶子也可以用来——

　　"好的,我知道了。"安妮打断杰克,放下篮子说:"我们现在就开始摇晃树干吧!"

　　杰克收好书,环顾四周,才发现树上挂着一簇簇棕色的水果。他抱住最近的一棵树,安妮从另一侧抱住。他们一起摇晃树干,直到有椰枣果掉下来。

　　在沙漠酷热的环境下,杰克和安妮从一棵树到另一棵树,不断摇晃树干,收集掉在地上的椰枣果。当他们装满两个大篮子时,棕榈树已经在绿洲上投下长长的影子。

　　杰克和安妮累得满头大汗。他们拖着沉甸甸的篮子去找商队的头领。他正在用篝火烧水。"啊,太棒了!"他说,"谢谢你们,安妮、杰克!"

　　"不用谢!"安妮说,"还有什么我们可以做的么?"

　　"你们现在需要休息。"他说,"愿意和我们一起喝茶吗?"

　　"当然愿意!"安妮说,"对了,您叫什么名字?"

　　"我的名字很长。"他笑着说,"你们可以叫我马姆。"

　　骆驼在旁边吃草,马姆和他的同伴把羊毛毯子铺在草地上,然后坐下来。他们和杰克、安妮一起品尝茶和椰枣果。这种黝黑丰满的水果很甜,也很有嚼头。茶很浓,但是很好喝。

在落日火红的余晖下，杰克注视着吃草的骆驼。他觉得这种背上驮着两个驼峰的动物非常有趣。它们长着毛茸茸的膝盖、笨拙的大脚和皱巴巴的小耳朵。它们喝水的时候会咂下嘴唇，吃草的时候嚼都不嚼就把一整束带刺儿的草吞下去。

"那些刺儿不会刺伤骆驼的喉咙吗？"杰克问马姆。

"不会的！"马姆回答，"它们的嘴巴非常坚硬。它们可以吃下任何东西，像骨头、棍子——"

"甚至是我们的帐篷和包裹，如果我们让它们吃的话！"另一个年轻的骆驼骑手补充道。

安妮和杰克都笑了。"你的包裹里面放的是什么？"安妮问。

"里面装着从希腊、土耳其和叙利亚带来的货物。"马姆回答,"里面有很多东西:宝石、珍珠和珍贵的香料,像桂皮、辣椒和香草。我们要把这些货物带到巴格达去卖。"

"我们也要去巴格达。"安妮说,"我们要去见哈里发。"

骆驼骑手们都哈哈大笑起来,好像安妮是在开玩笑一样。

只有马姆没有笑。"你们的家人是要去见哈里发吗?"他问。

"不!"安妮说,"只有杰克和我。我们要去帮助他向全世界传播智慧。"

"安妮!"杰克提醒她。

骆驼骑手们笑得更大声了。

"有这么好笑的么?"安妮问。

"哈里发是不接见小孩子的。"一个年轻人解释道,"他是这个世界上最有权利、最重要的人。"

"哦!"安妮皱了皱眉说。

这个消息让杰克非常担忧。

马姆好奇地看着杰克和安妮。"夜晚很快就要降临了。既然你们的家人还没有回来找你们,你们愿意和我们一起去巴格达吗?"他说,"你们已经骑着骆驼走了这么远,我相信你们也

能骑着骆驼走完剩下的路程。"

"当然可以！"安妮回答，"我们喜欢骆驼！"

是吗？杰克暗自思量着。

"好的，我们也很喜欢我们的沙漠之舟。"马姆说，"咱们一会儿就出发！"

"原来这就是沙漠之舟啊！"安妮悄悄地对杰克说。

啊，竟然是骆驼，天哪！杰克暗想。

沙漠之舟

Ships of the Desert

    "它非常适合在沙漠旅行。"马姆说,"它浓浓的眉毛可以遮挡刺眼的阳光,它长长的睫毛和耳朵边的毛发能抵御风吹起的沙尘。"

    "好神奇啊!"杰克轻声说。

骆驼骑手静静地注视着太阳落在远处的沙丘上。当那团红色的火球被地平线分成两半时，沙漠沉浸在红色的余晖中。终于，太阳完全消失在地平线以下，空气马上变得凉爽起来。

马姆站起来。"我们该走了！"他说。

几个骆驼骑手扑灭篝火。在越来越深的夜色中，马姆帮助他们整理好骆驼和行装。

然后他向杰克和安妮走去。"你们可以骑那一对骆驼姐妹。"他说着指向两只跪在沙漠上的骆驼，"爬上去吧，一会儿到队伍前面和我一起骑。"

安妮和杰克走向那对骆驼姐妹。它们的脖子上套着缰绳，高耸的驼峰上铺着彩色的坐垫。

安妮轻轻抚摸其中一只骆驼闪亮的棕色皮毛。那只骆驼忽闪着睫毛，用它的大眼睛看着安妮。"嗨，小可爱！"安妮和它打招呼。

另一只骆驼也蹭了蹭安妮的脖子。"嗨，小美丽！"安妮对它说。"你也希望我抚摸你吗？"

"小可爱？小美丽？"杰克质疑道。他没觉得那两只骆驼美丽或者可爱。

安妮爬上小可爱的彩色坐垫,拿起缰绳说:"我们出发吧!"

小可爱摇摇摆摆地从半跪的姿势站起来。"哦,哇!"安妮说。"它真的好高呀!"

杰克开始往小美丽的背上爬。但是小美丽咬住了他的头巾,开始咀嚼。

"别这样!"杰克说着从它嘴里抽出头巾。小美丽张开大大的嘴巴,露出两排锋利的牙齿。杰克忍不住往后退。

"别怕!"安妮说。

"你说得倒容易,"杰克说。"你的骆驼喜欢你!"

"不用担心,小美丽也喜欢你的!"安妮说,"我看得出来。"安妮的骆驼缓慢地向其它正在等待出发的骆驼走去。"快点,杰克!它走起路来可好玩儿了!"安妮鼓励杰克。

"好玩儿?"杰克嘟囔

着。"好吧！"他卷起头巾的一端，坐上小美丽的驼峰。小美丽好奇地看着杰克，然后甩甩尾巴，不停地拍打他的后背。

"嘿！"杰克说。

杰克想在坐垫上坐得舒服一些，但是小美丽的尾巴一直拍打他，还发出奇怪的叫声。

"安静点儿！"杰克把挎包挂在一个驼峰上。他好不容易坐好了。可是小美丽又转过头来，开始咀嚼他的挎包。

"哦，不，不要！"杰克叫喊着。他想把挎包拉回来，可是小美丽开始和他玩起了拔河。"快点，放开它，"杰克说，"别咬了，你这个蠢家伙！"

"你真的觉得它很蠢吗？"

马姆看见杰克试图从小美丽嘴里夺回挎包，就骑了过来。

杰克觉得有些尴尬。"它抢了我的东西。"杰克不好意思地说。

马姆拉起杰克挎包的背带，对小美丽发出几声咕咕的声音，小美丽就松口了。马姆再次把挎包挂在小美丽的驼峰上时，它只是轻声叫了一下。

"几千年来，向它这样的骆驼载着人们在沙漠里穿行。"马

姆说，"它真的是大自然的奇迹！"

只是奇迹之一而已，杰克暗想。

"它可以在十分钟内喝下两大桶水。"马姆接着说，"然后在沙漠里走上一星期都不用喝水。它还可以很多天不吃东西。"

"真的吗？"杰克问。

"它非常适合在沙漠旅行。"马姆说，"它浓浓的眉毛可以遮挡刺眼的阳光，它长长的睫毛和耳朵边的毛发能抵御风吹起的沙尘。"

"好神奇啊！"杰克轻声说。

"它的脚也很坚硬，感觉不到沙漠的火热，"马姆说，"而且它的脚非常大，所以它不会陷到松软的沙子里。"

"哦，"杰克感叹。

"它可以驮起五百磅重的行李。"马姆继续说，"它

一天就可以走几百英里。"

"好远啊！"杰克念叨。

马姆拉住骆驼的缰绳，打了个口哨。小美丽喘着粗气站起来，它强壮有力的长腿支撑起全部的重量。

马姆看着杰克。"我们必须尊敬爱护骆驼。"他说，"骆驼在很多方面都比我们优秀。"

杰克点点头。他想着梅林信中的话语。想要成功地完成任务，你们必须谦逊。他轻轻拍着骆驼说："小美丽，好孩子。"

马姆又打了个口哨，召集大家。杰克坐在高高的驼峰上，从一边晃到另一边。他觉得一点都不安全，但是他还是保持冷静。小美丽走到小可爱的身边，两姐妹站在一起，哼哼地说着话。

沙漠晴朗的夜空上挂着星星。马姆召集起所有的人，继续前进。

　　骆驼摇摇摆摆地向前走。它先同时移动一侧的两只大脚，再迈出另一侧的两只大脚。杰克紧紧地抓住小美丽的缰绳，因为他的沙漠之舟总是不停地左右来回摇摆。

　　"这难道不好玩儿吗？"安妮问。她也和杰克一样，左右晃来晃去。

　　"有点儿吧！"杰克说着抖了一下。实际上，他觉得这一点都不好玩儿。他觉得有点儿头晕，而且晚上的空气还有些冷。另外，他还在担心他们的任务。哈里发会接见他们吗？即使能见到哈里发，怎么样才能帮助他向世界传播智慧呢？如果巴格达离这里很远，他们怎么样才能找到回神奇树屋的路呢？

　　马姆赶上来，骑在杰克和安妮中间，放慢骆驼的脚步。"当

我还是个孩子的时候,有很多个寒冷的夜晚,我和父亲一起在沙漠里骑着骆驼去西方。"他说,"最开始,我也觉得骆驼很蠢。我总是希望可以在驼背上多垫一些毛毯,骑得舒服一些。我盼望着回到巴格达我那温暖的小床上。"

杰克笑了笑,他开始喜欢这个商队的头领了。

"但是随着时间的推移,我开始爱上这寒冷的沙漠之夜,"马姆说,"现在,当我躺在巴格达温暖的床上的时候,我又期盼着骑在驼背上,读着这里的风和星星。"

"你怎么能读懂星星呢?"安妮问。

"它们有自己的语言。"马姆回答,"比如现在,我们是在向东走,向着牡羊星的方向。"他指着天空说。

杰克不知道哪颗星星是牡羊星,但是他充满了好奇。黑色的穹幕上,数千颗星星在闪烁,多得超出杰克的想象。有些星星看上去伸手就可以摸到。

马姆开始唱歌,其他的骑手和他一起唱起来。杰克虽然听不懂他们在唱什么,但是曲调非常悠扬。骆驼们也好像在随着歌声摇摆。

杰克不再担心怎么样才能回到神奇树屋的事儿了。他发

现自己渐渐喜欢上了沙漠中清新的空气,心情也慢慢放松下来。

"杰克!"安妮轻声叫他,"想想看——我们刚刚解答了梅林信里的第一则谜语:在繁星满天的寒冷夜晚,乘坐沙漠之舟。"

"没错儿!"杰克高兴地说,"这真的很有趣!"

突然,远处传来尖锐的叫声。杰克坐直了身体,心怦怦直跳。

"强盗!"一个骆驼骑手惊呼。

5

强盗!

Bandits!

　　杰克环顾四周。只见沙漠里出现几个骑在马背上的黑色身影,正吼叫着朝他们所在的方向飞驰而来。

　　"哦!不!"杰克惊呼,"我们该怎么办?"

　　杰克环顾四周。只见沙漠里出现几个骑在马背上的黑色身影，正吼叫着朝他们所在的方向飞驰而来。

　　"哦！不！"杰克惊呼，"我们该怎么办？"

　　"我们会打败他们的！"马姆说，"你和安妮带上这个盒子去沙丘那边！"马姆说着从包里拿出一个扁平的木头盒子塞给杰克。"快走！用你们最快的速度离开这儿！用你们的生命保护这个盒子！"

　　杰克慌乱地想把盒子塞进挎包，但是马姆打了一下杰克骑的骆驼的屁股，然后骆驼突然奔跑起来。缰绳从杰克的手中滑脱了。杰克一手抓住驼峰，一手紧紧地把木盒子抱在胸口。小美丽带着杰克在黑暗的沙漠上奔驰。

　　安妮的骆驼与杰克的骆驼并驾齐驱，就像两匹赛马一样，向着远处的沙丘飞奔。杰克在驼背上剧烈地摇晃着，他紧紧地抱住盒子说："请——慢一点儿！"

　　但是没有用。小美丽像风一样地飞驰着。它和它的妹妹小可爱好像飞翔一般，越过星空下的沙漠。杰克想让骆驼停下来，但同时又希望远离那些强盗。

　　最后，两只骆驼终于放慢步伐。杰克回头去看，已经看不

到商队的影子,好像没有人跟过来。

两只骆驼来到沙丘旁,开始在沙丘的周围徘徊。它们找到一个可以隐蔽的安全的地方,停下来休息。小美丽嘟哝着,小可爱喷着鼻息。

"谢谢……谢谢!"安妮一边说一边抚摸着它们。

"我希望马姆和其他人都能安全!"杰克说。

"我也是。"安妮说,"他给我们的盒子里面装的是什么东西啊?"

杰克举起那个木盒子。"不知道!"他说,"但是马姆告诉我们,要用生命去保护它。"

"也许是珍贵的香料。"安妮说。

"希望不是。"杰克说,"我可不想为了桂皮或是辣椒搭上一条命。"

"我们可以看看吗?"安妮问。

"不知道!"杰克说,"马姆也许不想让我们看吧!"

"但是你不觉得,我们只有看了以后才能更好地保护它吗?"安妮说。

"或许吧……"杰克说。他明白安妮的意思,"好吧!"

　　杰克试图打开盒子但是打不开。黑暗之中,他摸到一个钥匙孔。"算了!"他说,"盒子是锁着的。"

　　"嘘!你听!"安妮说。

　　杰克听到一个尖锐的呻吟声,就像小提琴演奏的声音。那声音飘荡在干燥的沙丘上,越来越大。

　　"那是什么声音?"杰克问。

　　"哦——哇!"安妮突然说,"我又听到一个新的声音。"

　　杰克屏住呼吸。他听到蹄子在沙地上奔驰的声音。"是强盗!"他说。

　　"我们应该把盒子藏起来!"安妮说。

　　"藏在哪儿?"杰克问。

　　"藏在沙子里面!"安妮说。她打了声口哨,小可爱和小美丽都跪下来。杰克和安妮跳下坐垫,开始在沙地上挖坑。

　　蹄声越来越近了,杰克和安妮拼命地挖着。他们把沙子堆在身后,就像小狗刨坑一样地挖着。

　　"足够深了!"杰克说。他把木盒子放在坑里面,然后和安妮一起用挖出来的沙子把坑填上。

　　他们站起来以后,安妮喘着气说:"你瞧!"

　　在星光下，他们看到一个骑在骆驼上的黑影。他正飞快地越过沙丘向他们跑过来。杰克的心提到了嗓子眼儿。

　　"我们是不是该用魔法了？"安妮问杰克。

　　"我们已经没有时间了！"杰克说。

　　骑手越跑越近，最后直接停在杰克和安妮面前。"你们很安全，是吗？"他说。

　　"马姆！"安妮惊呼。

　　杰克顿时放下心来。他笑着说："是的，我们很安全！你们还好吧？"

　　"我的人很勇敢！"马姆说，"强盗只抢走了几袋辣椒和珍珠。"

　　"我们也保管好了你的盒子！"安妮说着蹲下来挖沙子，直到找到木盒子。她把盒子递给马姆。

　　"嗯，做得好！"商队头领赞扬道。

　　"盒子里面装的是什么呀？"安妮问。

　　"一件无价的珍宝，"马姆回答。"它是我一路从大马士革带回来的，我打算把它带回巴格达。谢谢你们用生命来保护它。你们真的很不简单！"

"不用谢！"杰克说。他还在想盒子里面装的到底是什么，是黄金？白银？还是珍贵的珠宝？

但是马姆没有解释。他重新把盒子放进自己的包里。"我们继续前进吧！"他说。

杰克爬上他那只跪在地上的骆驼。他打了个口哨，然后小美丽就伸长腿站了起来。杰克感到非常惊讶。

"我们会在巴格达追上其他人的。"马姆说，"如果一切顺利，我们预计会在下午到达巴格达。我们必须向着东方太阳升起的方向前进。"

马姆骑着骆驼离开沙丘，杰克和安妮跟在他后面。骆驼在寒冷的黎明中摇晃着。清晨的阳光逐渐亮起来，照耀着沙漠。

"马姆，昨天晚上我们在沙丘旁听到一个奇怪的声音。"安妮说，"就像演奏音乐的声音。"

"哦，没错儿！"马姆说，"那是'吹口哨的沙子'。"

"什么是'吹口哨的沙子'？"杰克问。

"有人说那是魔法。"马姆回答，"但是我认为大自然中的每一件事都有它发生的原因。这也是为什么我喜欢学习科学。科学说，我们必须观察这个世界，通过试验找到事情发生的原

因。我们发现那些口哨声是沙子落在沙丘上发出的声音。"

"哦！"安妮说，"可是我倒希望它是魔法。"

"研究事情发生的原因就是魔法。"马姆说，"真相可以给世界带来光明。这本来就是很奇妙的事情，难道不是吗？"

"是的。"杰克说。

安妮思索着点了点头。"如果你这么解释的话，应该就是了。"她说。

在清晨的沙漠里，他们三个人骑在骆驼上，摇来晃去地向前走着。但是不一会儿，太阳就出来了，高高地挂在天上。这时，沙漠变得炽热无比，干燥的风吹过沙漠，留下弯弯曲曲的痕迹。

马姆拉住他的骆驼，环顾四周，微微皱了皱眉。

"怎么了？"杰克询问，"又有强盗了吗？"

马姆摇了摇头。"不是强盗，现在是沙漠本身让我很烦恼。"他说，"我们没有地方可以休息。"他打了个口哨，骆驼又继续往前走。

他们在光秃秃的沙漠上走着，风把松散的沙子吹得满天都是。杰克和安妮低着头，以免风把沙子吹进眼睛。他们的头巾

在风中飞舞。越来越多的沙子被风扬起来。当沙子在空中飞舞时,整个沙漠就好像有了生命。

马姆再次停下来,环视四周。沙子形成的波浪的形状由弯弯曲曲变成了弧形。杰克听到了奇怪的呻吟声。"这次还是'吹口哨的沙子'吗?"他满怀期待地询问。

"不是!"马姆回答,"这次是可怕的沙暴的哭喊。它很快就会到我们这儿了。"

沙暴

Sandblasted

　　杰克用头巾使劲遮住脸，但是呼啸的大风一次次地把头巾吹起来。天空从红色变成了黑色，沙暴的声音也从低低的呻吟变成了隆隆的巨吼。

在远处，一层沙雾在沙漠上蔓延开。风向上吹起，天空变成了红色，沙雾变成了厚厚的棕色云团。云像一堵墙一样，慢慢地移动着，向杰克、安妮和马姆飞过来。

"快趴下！肚子贴地趴下！"马姆命令道，"快点！用头巾盖住脸！"

杰克打了个口哨，小美丽跪倒在地上。杰克、安妮和马姆跳下来，趴在骆驼旁边的沙子上。

杰克用头巾使劲遮住脸，但是呼啸的大风一次次地把头巾吹起来。天空从红色变成了黑色，沙暴的声音也从低低的呻吟变成了隆隆的巨吼。

杰克抬起头，看见风把马姆骆驼上的包裹吹起来，包裹掉在地上散开了。木盒子从包裹里掉出来，被大风刮走了。

"宝物！"杰克大叫一声，但是他的声音消失在风里。他跳起来，去追木盒。

杰克在沙漠上奔跑着，沙子打在他身上，风好像要把他吹倒。但是杰克用尽全力奔跑，直到他终于抓住木盒。他用身体压住木盒，拿起头巾的一端盖住脸。

沙暴吹打着杰克，听上去就好像上百只骆驼的蹄声。杰克

的眼睛火辣辣地疼,他觉得自己快要窒息了。

慢慢的,雷鸣变成隆隆声,隆隆声又渐渐变成呻吟声。风停息了。炽热的沙漠再次变得平静而安宁。

杰克翻个身,咳嗽着坐起来。他的嘴里、眼睛里、耳朵里和鼻子里全都是沙子。他取下眼镜,揉着刺痛的眼睛,可是好像越揉越疼!

杰克眨眨眼睛,抱紧木盒,四处寻找安妮和马姆的身影。空气中充斥着厚厚的沙尘,杰克完全迷失了方向。

"杰克!杰克!"
他听见安妮的喊声。

杰克握住木盒,
努力站起来。他的腿
一点力气都没有,又
跌倒在地上。"安妮!"
杰克大声喊。

"杰克!"安妮的声音穿过厚厚的沙尘。"你在哪儿?"

"我在这儿!"杰克回答。

"哪儿?"

"这儿！"

"原来你在这儿！"安妮说着冲了过来，"你还好吗？"

"我还好！"杰克说，"你呢？"

"还好！我一直跟在你后面跑。"安妮说。她的声音听上去也是沙哑的。

"我是在追木盒。"杰克说，"马姆在哪儿呢？"

"我也不知道！"安妮说，"他可能没看见咱们俩去追木盒。"

"马姆！"他俩一起呼喊。"马姆！"

但是没有回应。

透过沙雾，杰克听见一阵蹄声。他和安妮转过身，看到他们的两只骆驼正向他们跑过来。

"小可爱！"安妮呼唤道，"小美丽！"

杰克和安妮跑向两只骆驼，抓住它们的缰绳。

"谢谢你们来找我们！"杰克一边说一边抚摸

着小美丽。

"马姆！"安妮继续叫喊，"马姆！"

"他也许是去了相反的方向找我们，"杰克说。

"如果找不到他，我们怎么去巴格达啊？还有他的宝物该怎么办呢？"安妮问。

"我也不知道，"杰克说着举起那个木盒子。

"瞧，盒子打开了！"安妮指着盒盖子上的一条大裂缝说。

"希望里面的宝物没被弄坏。"杰克说。

"也许我们应该打开检查一下。"安妮说。

杰克深吸一口气。他一直觉得马姆不希望他们看到盒子里面的宝物。但是他实在忍不住自己的好奇心。"好吧。"他说，"咱们只是看看宝物有没有被弄坏，应该没关系吧！"

杰克取下盒盖儿上的两片木头，发现盒子里面是一本书。

"书？"杰克惊奇地说。他原本以为盒子里装的是金子或珠宝。他小心翼翼地把书拿出来。书的封面是皮子做的，但是上面没有书名。

"它看上去不像是什么宝物呀！"安妮说。

"也许里面记录的东西是宝物。"杰克分析道。

杰克轻轻地打开书。里面黄色的纸张非常厚，是用线缝起来的。纸的正反两面都写着字。第一页上写着：

亚里士多德的著作

"谁是亚里士多德呀？"安妮拼读出这个名字问。

"我也不知道！"杰克说，"我到指导书里查一查。"他从驼峰上取下挎包，沙子盖住了书。杰克取出指导书，拂去上面的沙子。他在目录中查找亚里士多德。"找到了，在这儿！"杰克说。他翻到那一页，读道：

　　亚里士多德生活在 2300 多年前的古希腊。

　　他被喻为历史上最伟大的哲学家之一。哲学家一词的本意是"爱智慧的人"。

　　亚里士多德的著作在中世纪时由阿拉伯人传入西方国家。

　　"这么说,亚里士多德就是一个非常爱智慧的人啦!"安妮说。

　　"我想是的!"杰克说,"但是我在想,为什么这本书如此珍贵呢?"

　　"等一下!"安妮说,"梅林在信里面不是说,我们要帮助哈里发向世界传播智慧吗?"

　　杰克惊叹一声说道:"对啊!还有,如果这是亚里士多德的著作的话,那里面一定充满了智慧……我们应该把这本书带

给哈里发——这就是我们这次的梅林任务！"

"咱们赶快出发吧！"安妮说。

杰克和安妮握住缰绳，打了个口哨。小可爱和小美丽跪倒在沙地上，杰克和安妮爬到它们背上。杰克丢掉那个已经坏了的木盒子，小心翼翼地把亚里士多德的著作和指导书一起放进挎包，然后把挎包挂在驼峰上。

"应该朝哪个方向走呢？"安妮问。

"向着太阳升起的东方！"杰克回答，"马姆是这么告诉我们的。"

"那就是这个方向了。"安妮指着远处天边的一抹亮光说。

在漫天的沙尘里，杰克和安妮的骆驼面向耀眼的太阳前进着。"嘿，我们现在正在执行梅林的第二条指示。"安妮说，"乘坐它穿过沙尘和酷热的早晨。"

"没错儿！"杰克说。

杰克和安妮一直向着东方行进。炽热的沙子泛着光，四周的视野变得清晰起来，但是他们还是没有看到马姆的踪影。

杰克低下头，避开耀眼的阳光。他疲惫地闭上眼睛。小美丽轻轻地摇晃着，杰克耷拉的脑袋也摇晃着。突然，他听到安

妮大喊一声："杰克！快看！"

"什么？是马姆吗？"杰克猛地惊醒了。

"不是的！你瞧！"安妮说。

在远方晴朗的天空下,杰克看见一片塔尖和屋顶在阳光下闪烁着。"哦,天哪！"他轻呼一声。"是巴格达！"

第三堵墙的后面

Behind the Third Wall

　　小美丽和小可爱载着杰克和安妮穿过第三道城门，来到巴格达的中心。一座宫殿出现在他们的眼前。在宫殿绿色的屋顶上，矗立着一匹马的雕塑。

小美丽和小可爱继续向巴格达前进，脚下松软的沙子渐渐变成被太阳晒裂的土地。又过了一会儿，干裂的土地渐渐变成稀疏的草地。山羊和绵羊在吃草，旁边还有星星点点的农田。

不一会儿，杰克和安妮就来到了一条红土铺成的路上。那条路一直延伸到一个十字路口。来自四面八方的商人聚集在路口，准备去巴格达。杰克和安妮看到旁边有小男孩儿在放羊，有农民驾着驴车经过，还有戴着面纱的妇女在肩上扛着大瓶子走过。

杰克还在寻找马姆，但是仍然没有看到他的身影。他们随着人流往前走。小美丽和小可爱跨过一座桥。桥下有划艇和游船在黄褐色的河面上航行。

河对岸是一个巨大的露天市场。好像很多来自不同国家的人正在那儿做买卖。空气中洋溢着香料的味道。摊位周围堆满了麻袋、篮子和地毯。鞋匠跷着二郎腿在那儿做鞋。陶匠靠在火炉边烧制土黄色的器皿。纺织工匠坐在小巧的织布机前编织丝绸的锦缎。

"卖纸、卖珍珠咯！"一位商人喊道。

"我们不买，谢谢！"安妮说。

"要鸽子、鹦鹉吗？"另一个商人问杰克。

"不要,谢谢！"杰克回答。

"我喜欢这儿！"安妮说。"这儿是什么地方？"

"我来查查,"杰克说着拿出指导书,读道:

> 在九世纪,世界各地的商人把货
> 物带到巴格达来交易。
>
> 巴格达的商人用纸张、上好的布
> 料和珠宝交换来自西班牙、印度、非
> 洲、中国、希腊和其他地方的货物。
>
> 这些交易在一个叫做巴扎尔的
> 露天市场进行。

"哦,这么说,巴扎尔就相当于一个大超市了。"杰克说。

"这儿比大超市好多了！"安妮反驳道,"我们下去看看吧！"

"我们没有时间去购物。"杰克说,"我们要去完成任务。"

他拿出梅林的信读道:

> 在屋顶上找到一匹马，
> 它可以看见所有的东西。
> 它在市中心第三堵墙的后面。

"听上去好像我们走过三堵墙就能看到一匹马。"杰克说，"那么，我们还是继续走吧！"

杰克收起书和信。小美丽和小可爱在嘈杂的巴扎尔集市穿行。他们走出巴扎尔后，看到一堵弯曲的砖砌的墙。墙脚是泥做的城壕。

"瞧——这一定是第一堵墙！"安妮说。

"太棒了！"杰克说。

杰克和安妮骑着骆驼走过跨在城壕上的拱桥，然后穿过有两扇铁门的城楼。城墙的另一边是一条楼房林立的繁华街道。

他们的骆驼在人群中穿行。杰克取出指导书，一边摇晃着，一边读道：

在黄金时代，巴格达有很好的医院。

这座城市同样因为它良好的政治制度、公立学校、大量的图书馆和商店以及养着上百头狮子的动物园而闻名。

"我想去动物园看一下那些狮子。"安妮说。

"我们现在没有时间去那儿。"杰克解释道。

他们的骆驼穿过繁忙的街道，来到一块绿地。

"你瞧，第二堵墙！"安妮说。

只见绿地四周围着一堵墙。这堵墙也是弯曲的，但是比第一堵墙高很多，看上去至少有一百英尺高。城门口有人守卫，但是他们似乎不盘查过往的行人。

"表现得正常一些。"杰克对安妮说，"不要引起他们的注意。"

杰克和安妮混入人流，顺利通过城门。第二堵墙的后面是

另一条大街。街道很宽阔，它的尽头是另一片绿地。"你瞧，第三堵墙！"安妮说。

第三堵墙比第二堵墙还要高。同样，行人可以自由出入。

"这部分任务很简单呀！"安妮说。

"没错儿！"杰克说，"但是我们还要去找屋顶上的马，然后再找到哈里发，让他接见我们。"

小美丽和小可爱载着杰克和安妮穿过第三道城门，来到巴格达的中心。一座宫殿出现在他们的眼前。在宫殿绿色的屋顶上，矗立着一匹马的雕塑。

"啊，能看见一切的马！"安妮惊呼。"我敢打赌，哈里发就住在这宫殿里面。"她指向宫殿长廊外的拱门。很多人正走向拱门。

杰克和安妮穿过拱门，走进一个美丽的花园。空气中洋溢着花的芳香。他们走过一条棕榈树环绕的小路，来到一个院子里。一个小男孩儿正在院子里玩秋千。院子旁边有供骆驼休息的棚子。

"看来接下来的路我们得自己走了。"杰克说。

"是的，我想我们可以把小美丽和小可爱留在那儿。"安妮

指着旁边的棚子说。

杰克和安妮来到棚子边,打了个口哨,两只骆驼就跪下来。杰克去取挎包时,一个球滚到棚子里。安妮捡起球,走出棚子。杰克跟在她后面也走出来。

"这儿!"一个长着一头黑色卷发的小男孩儿喊道。他伸出手,安妮把球扔过去,他接住球。他笑着称赞安妮扔球扔得好。"你们是谁?"他问。"你们从哪儿来?"

杰克还没得及回答,安妮已经向那群男孩子走去,杰克快速追上她。

"我是安妮,这是我的哥哥杰克。"安妮回答,"我们来自宾夕法尼亚的蛙溪湾。"

"你们为什么来巴格达呢?"男孩子接着问。

"我们是来找哈里发的。"安妮回答。

那孩子和他的同伴都笑了。

"有什么好笑的?"安妮问。

"我们的哈里发是这个世界上最有权势的人。"另一个孩子解释,"他是没有时间接见小孩子的。"

"人们一直都这么说。"安妮说,"但是我们来这儿有很重

要的任务。我们——"

"安妮！"杰克打断她的话，"快过来，我把书包忘在棚子里了。"他向那群小男孩儿挥手道别："再见！安妮，快走！"

安妮跟着杰克离开。

"如果你们找到哈里发以后他不接见你们，就回来和我们一起玩球吧！"长着卷发的那个男孩儿说。

安妮停下来说："别担心，他会接见我们的！我们不是普通的小孩子！"

"安妮，快过来！"杰克喊道。

"你们有什么不普通的呢？"那个男孩子穷追不舍。

"首先，我们刚刚冒着沙暴从强盗手中拯救了一件宝物。"安妮说，"其次——"

"安妮！"杰克焦急地制止安妮。他抓住安妮的胳膊，把她拉到身边："过来！"

他们回到放骆驼的棚子以后，杰克摇着头说："以后不要再这样说了。"

"为什么呢？"安妮问。

"因为这是吹嘘。"杰克回答，"这会让其他的孩了觉得自

卑，即使你真的很特别，你也没有必要去——"

"哦，不！"安妮突然哭喊起来。她忍不住用手捂住嘴巴。

"怎么了？"杰克看着她惊讶的表情说。

杰克的挎包落在小美丽的脚边，包里的东西都散开了。旁边是亚里士多德的著作的封面，书已经被踩烂了。小美丽正津津有味地咀嚼这这件珍贵的宝物，潮湿的纸片还挂在它的嘴角边。

有树的房间

Room of the Tree

　　杰克转过身，看到一棵巨大的树立在房间的正中央。它银色的叶子闪动着，好像有风吹过一样。在银色的树叶中间，有机械鸟在咯吱咯吱地歌唱。

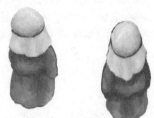

"不——！"杰克大喊起来。

杰克冲向小美丽，试图把残留的纸片从它嘴里抽出来。安妮跪在地上，拾起落在小美丽脚边的一片一片破碎的书页。

"宝物被毁坏了！"安妮叹息道。

杰克被吓呆了。"我不应该把挎包留在这儿的！"他懊恼地说。

"不，这都是我的错。我不应该走过去向那些孩子吹嘘。"安妮哀叹道，"我应该表现得更加谦逊，就像梅林说的那样。"安妮听上去好像要哭了。

"没关系！"杰克安慰她。但是杰克自己也知道，他们现在有大麻烦了。书被毁了，他们也许无法完成这次的任务了。

"也许——也许我们可以修好它。"安妮说。

杰克摇摇头说："不行，我们修不好了。它已经完全被毁坏了，再也修不好了。"

安妮抬起头。"什么？你刚才说什么？"

"我说它修不好了。"杰克重复道。

安妮的脸上突然露出一个大大的笑容。"对！这本书不能修好了！"她说。"帮我把所有这些碎片都收集起来！"

"为什么？"杰克问。安妮是不是中邪了？

"照我说的做！快点！"安妮说。

杰克和安妮在棚子里忙着收集书的碎片。

"现在把所有的碎片都堆在书的封面上，再把那本书给我，"安妮命令道。

"什么书？"杰克问。

"魔法口诀书！"安妮说。

"哦，对啊！"杰克惊呼一声。"没错儿！"他从背包里取出泰德和凯思琳的魔法口诀书。

杰克打开书，顺着目录读下来。"在这儿：修好不能修好的东西，"他说。

"就是这个！"安妮说。

杰克飞快地翻到那一页。他举起书，这样他和安妮都可以看见。他们站在阳光下，杰克用清晰而洪亮的声音念道：

修好不能修好的东西！

安妮接着念第二行的海豹语：

> 啊喂-布哩-奥！费恩-啊-吗来！

纸片开始飞舞，它们在地面上旋转，接着又飞到空中，四周好像有一股小型的龙卷风。龙卷风把所有的纸片都集中到一起，形成一个漏斗的形状。纸片的旋涡中间有一束耀眼的光芒。

杰克遮住眼睛，然后听到一声巨响。当他睁开眼睛时，耀眼的龙卷风已经消失了。

在安妮和杰克的面前，那本古老的书就静静地躺在棚子的地板上。

杰克屏住呼吸，小心**翼翼**地从地上拿起那件宝物。他打开书的封面，惊叹道："哦，天哪！"亚里士多德充满智慧的话语工工整整地出现在泛黄的纸张上，没有一点折过或是撕过的痕迹。

"谢天谢地!"安妮感叹一声。

"是啊!"杰克也忍不住感叹。

"那么接下来我们该怎么办呢?"杰克自言自语道,"梅林给我们的下一个指示是什么呢?"他取出梅林的信念道:

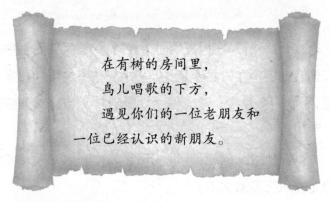

在有树的房间里,

鸟儿唱歌的下方,

遇见你们的一位老朋友和

一位已经认识的新朋友。

"这是什么意思呢?"杰克说。

突然,杰克听见身后有人。他和安妮转过身,看见一位穿着白色长袍的女孩子正站在棚子的门口。她的脸和头发都被纱巾遮住了。

"你好!"安妮和她打招呼,"你是谁?"

"我是宫里的仆人。"女孩儿小声说,"跟我来!"

她示意杰克和安妮跟她走。

"咱们跟她走吧！"安妮对杰克说。

"她要把我们带到哪里去呢？"杰克问，"还有，她为什么说话那么小声啊？"

"我也不知道。"安妮说，"但是我觉得我们应该跟她走。"

"好吧。"杰克说。他把亚里士多德的智慧书和那本魔法书都放进挎包，然后背上挎包，跟着安妮和那位女仆走出棚子。

他们三人走过庭院，穿过宫门。他们踩着厚厚的羊毛地毯，穿过被蜡烛照亮的长廊。

在长廊的尽头有一扇高高的雕花大门。一个男仆站在门边，他穿着宽松的裤子和长衫，脸完全被头巾遮住了。他不看杰克他们三人，也不和他们说话。

女仆站得离杰克和安妮很近。她用奇怪的声音轻轻地对他们说："在椅子前面，低下身子，不要抬头看，也不要说话，直到有人和你们说话。"

"但是——"杰克说。

"快去！"女仆小声催促。

男仆打开那扇厚重的门，女仆把他们推了进去。

"等等！"杰克说。

但是太迟了，男仆已经把他们身后的门关上了，只留下杰克和安妮。

"杰克，瞧！我们找到了！"安妮说。"有树的房间！"

杰克转过身，看到一棵巨大的树立在房间的正中央。它银色的叶子闪动着，好像有风吹过一样。在银色的树叶中间，有机械鸟在咯吱咯吱地歌唱。

在那棵奇怪的树下面，有一张黑色的椅子，上面镶嵌着闪闪发光的珠宝。

"就是这个地方！"安妮说着念起梅林信中的话：

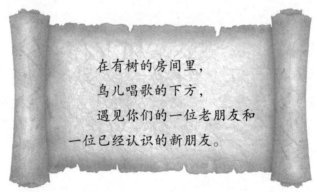

在有树的房间里，
鸟儿唱歌的下方，
遇见你们的一位老朋友和
一位已经认识的新朋友。

"又解决了一个问题。"安妮说。

"还没解决呢。"杰克说，"那两位朋友在哪里呢？"

"我也不知道，但是我们最好在椅子前面跪下，按照那个女仆说的做。"安妮建议。

杰克和安妮在那把闪亮的椅子前面跪下，弯下身子，脑袋贴着地面。杰克紧紧地抱着装着宝物的挎包。

"别忘了，她还说过，不要抬头看，也不要说话，直到有人和你们说话。"安妮嘱咐杰克。

"但是这儿并没有人啊！"杰克说。他觉得跪在椅子前面听机械鸟唱歌非常愚蠢。我们为什么要这么做呢？他思索着。

正在这时，咯吱一声门被打开了。杰克闭上眼睛，听见有脚步声逐渐向他们走来。

"你们是怎么进来的？"一个深沉而粗暴的声音问。

"是一位仆人带我们进来的。"安妮回答。

"那你们为什么要进来呢？"那个声音接着问。

"我们有珍贵的礼物要献给巴格达的哈里发。"杰克回答，但是不敢抬头。"是一本充满智慧的书。"

杰克打开挎包，取出那本书。然后，他继续闭着眼睛，把书朝那个声音的方向递过去。

接下来是很长时间的沉默。

"我们希望它可以帮助哈里发向世界传播智慧。"安妮说。

"你们是怎么得到这本书的？"那个人问。

"我们是在帮助一位朋友。"安妮回答，"我们和他在沙暴中走散了。"

"哦，那么你们把书带到巴格达是想得到奖赏啦？"那个人说。

"不！不是的！"杰克连忙回答，"我们的任务就是把书交给哈里发。"

"你们一定是想用这本书来交换什么东西。"那个人说，"你们难道不想得到从甜美花瓣上收集来的香水吗？"

"我们不要，谢谢！"安妮回答。

"那么你们想要和鸡蛋一样大的红宝石么？"那个人接着问。

"我们也不要，谢谢！"杰克回答。

"那么你们要不要和这本书一样重的黄金呢？"那个人问。

"我们真的不需要奖赏！"杰克说。

"如果哈里发那么喜欢书，那么你们为什么不告诉他，让他用他的金子和宝石去多买些书呢？"安妮问。

　　他们又一次陷入了沉默。然后，那个人清了清嗓子。当他再次说话时，传来的是一个温柔而又熟悉的声音。"抬起头来看着我，杰克和安妮，"他说。

　　杰克睁开眼睛，慢慢地抬起头。一开始他看见的是金灿灿的靴子……然后是镶着金边的白色长袍……然后是一张熟悉的脸。

　　杰克倒吸一口凉气。他真不敢相信自己的眼睛。站在他们面前的不是一个凶巴巴的陌生人，而是他们的朋友马姆！

智慧之屋

House of Wisdom

　　"你们向我展现了对书籍和知识的热爱与崇敬。"哈里发说，"你们同时也表现了一颗谦逊的心。在你们回到家人身边之前，我想带你们去一个非常特别的地方。我把它叫做智慧之屋。"

"马姆？"安妮惊讶地喊道。

"是我！"马姆回答，"看到你们平安地来到巴格达，我很高兴。"

"看到你一切都好，我们也很高兴！"安妮说，"我们一直还担心你呢！"

"沙暴过后，我到处寻找你们。"马姆说，"最后我放弃了，伤心地回到了巴格达。我想你们已经找到家人了，是吗？"

"嗯，当然！"安妮回答，"我们找到他们了。"

"而且我们还找到了你的书。"杰克接着说，"我们发现找不到你以后，就决定把这本书带给哈里发。"

马姆微笑地说："你们还不明白，是吗？"

"明白什么？"安妮问。

"我就是哈里发·阿布拉哈·马姆。"

"你就是哈里发？"安妮惊讶地说。

"但是——怎么——为什么？"杰克结结巴巴地说。

"多年以来，我一直希望找到一本介绍亚里士多德的智慧的书。"哈里发解释，"我听说在大马士革可以找到这样的书，于是就想为我的图书馆收藏一本。最关键的是，要把书安全地

带回来。另外，我很怀念小时候在沙漠上旅行的日子。所以，我就扮作一个普通的商人，来完成这次旅行。我的同伴都不知道我是哈里发。"

"哇！"杰克轻轻感叹一声。

"你们向我展现了对书籍和知识的热爱与崇敬。"哈里发说，"你们同时也表现了一颗谦逊的心。在你们回到家人身边之前，我想带你们去一个非常特别的地方。我把它叫做智慧之屋。"

"智慧之屋？"杰克兴奋地喊道，"好酷的名字啊！"

"我希望全世界都能发现它的奇妙之处。"哈里发说，"跟我来！"他说着走出房间。杰克和安妮从地上站起来，跟在他后面快速地往外走。

哈里发拿着亚里士多德的著作，带着杰克和安妮走出有树的房间。他走下台阶时，那件镶着金边的白袍在他的身边飞舞。每一个经过的人都跪在地上，向他行礼。

"又一个谜底被解开了！"安妮对杰克说。她引用梅林信中的原话说道：

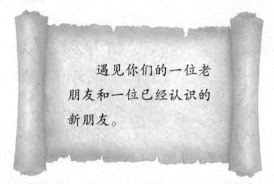

遇见你们的一位老朋友和一位已经认识的新朋友。

"两个朋友是同一个人！"安妮继续说，"沙漠中遇到的马姆和哈里发·阿布拉哈·马姆。"

"没错儿！"杰克笑着说。

哈里发带着杰克和安妮走出宫殿的大门，来到外面的庭院中。院子里站着两只骆驼，骆驼背上系着长长的杆子，长杆上面坐着一顶小轿子，轿子的四角装饰着金色的穗子和黄铜做的铃铛。

仆人们扶着杰克、安妮和哈里发爬上那顶奇怪的小轿子。两只骆驼穿过庭院时，轿子上的铃铛叮咚作响。

哈里发打开轿子上的一扇小门，让空气和阳光透进来。杰克向外面看去。每一个人看见皇家的轿子经过时，都低下头行礼，包括玩球的小男孩、浇水的花匠和顶着瓶子的妇女。

杰克对智慧之屋有很多的疑问，但是他不知道哈里发是否愿意回答，所以不好意思问。就连安妮在他们经过棕榈树和宫殿的花园时也没有说话。

"我们到了。"哈里发说。骆驼停了下来，哈里发扶着杰克和安妮从轿子上下来，然后带着他们走向一栋砖砌的建筑。

"欢迎来到智慧之屋。"哈里发说，"这儿是全世界的学习中心。"

"这儿是用来做什么的呢？"杰克询问。

"跟我来，我告诉你们。"哈里发领着杰克和安妮穿过前门，沿着长廊往里走。"这儿有一个用来研制新药物的实验室，"他介绍道，"还有一个专门用来观测星象的观测室。但是，这个房间才是我最喜欢的。"

　　哈里发在一个拱门前停下来。他打开门，带着杰克和安妮走进一个巨大而安静的房间。"这里就是图书馆。"他压低声音说，"就算是我来到这里也必须保持安静。"

　　午后的阳光从高大的窗户洒进来，落在书架和彩色的书本封面上。人们坐在长长的桌子边读书。他们抬头看到哈里发以后，都站了起来。

　　"你们继续，不要在意我。"哈里发轻声说。

　　他们又坐下来继续读书写字。

　　哈里发指向窗户边一位长着胡子的人。高高堆起的书把他包围在中间，他正在奋笔疾书。

　　"那是阿库瓦日子米。"哈里发悄声说，"他是一位伟大的数学家。他改进了印度的数字的书写方法。"哈里发指着墙上的数字：1、2、3、4、5、6、7、8、9、10。"我们把这叫做阿拉伯数字。"他说。

　　"阿拉伯数字？"杰克疑惑地问。

"没错儿！"哈里发回答。

杰克小声对安妮说："我们用的也是阿拉伯数字，就是那个人发明的呀？"

哈里发指着窗户边的另一个人说："他是金迪。他或许是这个世界上最伟大的科学家和思想家。"哈里发低声说，"但是他很谦虚。他认为知识不应该只属于某一个人或某一个国家，而是应该属于全世界。只有广泛地传播智慧，世界才会变得更美好。这也是我的观点。正因为如此，我才修建了这个图书馆。"

"我也赞成他的观点。"安妮小声说。

"我也是。"杰克附和道。

"来自世界各国的科学家和学者在这里读书、学习，分享他们的智慧。"哈里发说，"我们这里有上千本手抄书。"

"手抄书？"安妮惊讶地说，"那得写好多字呀！"

"都有什么书？"杰克问。

"有关于历史、数学、地理和医学的书。"哈里发回答，"还

有一本介绍奇迹和神话的书。"

　　哈里发从书架上取下一本又大又厚的
书。他把书放在桌子上，展示给杰克和安妮
看。书是用漂亮的手写体写成的。书里有
阿拉丁、阿里巴巴、神灯和飞毯的图画。

　　"哦，《阿拉伯的神话故事》！"安妮说，
"我们知道这些故事。"

　　"是吗？太神奇了！"哈里发笑着说。
"也许是我们这儿的人旅行到了你们那儿，
在途中传播了这些故事。说不定我们从你
们那儿带来的故事很快也会传播开来。书
的力量是无穷的，你们说是吗？"

　　"是的！"安妮回答。

　　"我希望你们那儿的人也听说过这本书的故事。"哈里发
说着拿起亚里士多德的著作，"等我读完以后，我会让人抄写
几本，把智慧传播到全世界。非常感谢你们的帮助！"

　　"不客气！"杰克坚定地说，"这是我们的任务！"

　　"我想我该去履行我的义务了。"哈里发说，"不过，你们回

家之前可以一直呆在这里看书。以后别忘了回来看我哦！"

"我们会的。"杰克说。

"再见，安妮。再见，杰克。"

"再见，马姆。"安妮说。

和蔼的哈里发给了他们一个温和的微笑，同时深深地鞠了一躬，然后就离开了杰克和安妮，还有他那神奇的图书馆。

在月亮升起之前

Before the Moon Rises

"记住,生活充满了奇迹!"安妮重复梅林信中的话。

"是的,在月亮升起之前回到树屋。"杰克接着安妮的话补充了后面的两句。

杰克和安妮环顾大房间的四周，发现各位学者和科学家都沉浸在他们的阅读之中。

"真不敢相信马姆就是哈里发。"杰克低声说。

"记住，生活充满了奇迹！"安妮重复梅林信中的话。

"是的，在月亮升起之前回到树屋。"杰克接着安妮的话补充了后面的两句。

"我差点儿把这句给忘了！"安妮说。

"我也是。"杰克说。

"嘘！"一位学者说。

"对不起！"安妮连忙道歉。

杰克和安妮向窗外的天空望去。天空变成了粉红色，太阳就要下山了。"咱们必须赶快回树屋。"安妮小声说，"在月亮升起之前。"

"我知道。"杰克说，"可是现在怎么回去啊？"他觉得有些惊慌。他想，树屋真的在很远的地方，即使骑着小美丽和小可爱回去，大概也要花一整天的时间。如果再遇上沙暴或是强盗该怎么办呢？杰克转头去看安妮。

她笑了，然后用唇语说，魔法。

杰克摇着头长舒一口气。他们环顾一下四周,看有没有学者或科学家注意到他们,发现没有人在看他们。

杰克悄悄地把凯思琳和泰德的魔法书从包里拿出来。他和安妮背对着其他人,打开书的目录。

安妮指了指"变成鸭子"这一条口诀。

杰克摇了摇头。

安妮又指了指"在天空飞行"这一条。

"就是这条!"杰克说。

"嘘!"一位学者发出一声抱怨。

杰克翻到那一页,然后举起书,让他俩都可以看见。

杰克念出口诀的第一行:

飞过天空,去你想去的地方。

安妮念出下一行:

萨温-哧-佛哩，萨温-哧-罗唔！

"你们俩安静一点儿，要不然就赶快离开这个图书馆！"一位学者不满地说。

"别着急，我们马上就离开。"安妮回答。

透过敞开着的高高的窗户，一阵风吹进屋里，吹动着《阿拉伯的神话故事》的书页。那些学者和科学家抢着去抓纸张，怕风把它们吹跑。

风卷起杰克和安妮站着的那块地毯的一角。地毯被拉起来，杰克和安妮摔倒在上面。他们还没来得及站起来，地毯已经飞离了地面。

"哦！"学者和科学家们叫喊着。

地毯开始向上升，一直升到比长桌子还要高，然后越过书架。所有人都从椅子上跳起来，喊叫着："小心！"——"这不可能！"——"快走！"——"救命啊！"——"怎么回事儿啊？"

“再见！”安妮说。

地毯飞向着敞开着的高高的窗户，透过窗户飞出了智慧之屋。

寒冷的风吹打着杰克和安妮。地毯载着他们在天空上飞行。他们的头巾在空中疯狂地飞舞。

“太棒了！”杰克大声欢呼。

“真的很不错！”安妮大声叫喊。

地毯飞过智慧之屋，飞过正在回宫殿的路上的哈里发，飞过骆驼休息的棚子。

地毯飞过矗立着马的雕像的绿色屋顶，飞过孩子在玩球的庭院，飞过第三堵墙、绿地和街道。

地毯飞过第二堵墙、房屋、医院和养着上百头狮子的动物园，飞过第一堵墙、拱桥和城壕。

地毯飞过鞋匠、陶匠和纺织工匠聚集的巴扎尔集市，飞过通向巴格达的道路。杰克和安妮低下头看到路上驾着驴车的农夫、放羊的小男孩和顶着瓶子的妇女。

地毯越飞越快——

越过小河和牧场，

和会吹口哨的沙子，

越过炽热的沙漠

向着落日

和那片陌生的

小小绿洲飞去。

神奇的地毯在一眼泉水旁边的绿地上停下来，绿地旁边就是棕榈树和绳梯。

沙漠看上去就像燃烧的火一样闪着金红色的光芒。杰克感觉头晕眼花。"这——这也太快了吧！"他说，"真不敢相信我们就这样回来了！"

"我们真的回来了。"安妮说，"是魔法帮助了我们。"

她和杰克试着站起来。他们摇摇晃晃地又倒了下去。

"站稳了。"安妮咯咯地笑着说，"你还好吧？"

"很好！"杰克回答。他把挎包挂在肩膀上，走下地毯。然后，他和安妮向那棵最高的棕榈树走去。杰克从树干后面取出绳梯，开始和安妮往上爬。

他们钻进树屋后，杰克取出梅林的信，最后一次望向窗外。

太阳已经下山了。地毯在棕榈树的影子里，看上去非常渺

小，非常普通。沙漠看上去也是一片寂静和孤独。一轮新月升上天空。

"在月亮升起之前回到树屋。"杰克说。

"这是梅林给我们的最后一个指示。"安妮说，"我们都做到了。"

杰克看着梅林的信，指着"蛙溪湾的杰克和安妮"几个字说："我希望我们可以回家！"

风开始刮了起来。

树屋开始旋转。

它越转越快。

然后一切都静止了。

完全静止了。

＊　＊　＊

午后蛙溪湾的树林有些寒冷。杰克和安妮穿着牛仔裤和夹克。

"不错的旅行！"杰克简单地评价道。

安妮点点头说："真的非常棒！"

"我想我们该回家了。"杰克说，"我还有很多作业要做呢！"

"把指导书留下,但是别忘了带上泰德和凯思琳的魔法口诀书。"安妮说。

杰克从背包里取出关于巴格达黄金时代的书,放在树屋的地板上。然后,他又背上背包,开始下绳梯,安妮跟在后面。他们一起穿过早春的树林。

"我们通过了梅林的第二次考验。"安妮说,"我们帮助哈里发向世界传播了文化……这真是件了不起的事。"

"要谦虚!"杰克提醒安妮。

"嗯,我觉得泰德和凯思琳的魔法书在困难的时候给了我们不少帮助。"安妮谦虚地说。

"我想他们了。"杰克说。

"我也是。"安妮说。"但是我觉得在巴格达的时候他们也许和我们在一起。"

"你指的是什么?"杰克说。

"还记得那个带我们去见哈里发的女仆和男仆吗?"安妮解释。"他们不知道从哪里就冒出来了。而且我们都没有看到他们的脸,是不是?"

"嗯,没看到……"杰克说。"你觉得?"

安妮耸耸肩。"也许吧!"

杰克笑着深吸一口气,轻声说:"也许是吧!"

"还剩下两个任务和五条魔法口诀。"安妮说。"我希望梅林很快就会再来找我们。"

"但不要太快。"杰克说,"我还要先把作业做完。"

安妮大笑一声,然后问道:"是有阿拉伯数字的数学题吗?"

"没错儿!"杰克回答,"也许明天我们可以去图书馆找找有没有介绍亚里士多德智慧的书。"

"好主意!"安妮赞许道。

一阵早春的寒风吹动了树叶。在寒风里,杰克和安妮快速向家里赶去。

可怕的沙尘暴

● 巴格达是一座古老的城市,位于底格里斯河和幼发拉底河之间。很久以前,这里被叫做美索不达米亚,意思就是"在两河之间"。现在这块土地被叫做伊拉克,巴格达是它的首都。

● 哈伦·拉·希德开启了一个黄金时代。他使巴格达在接下来的四百多年成为文化和知识的中心。1258 年,这座城市被入侵的蒙古骑兵毁灭。

● 智慧之屋是东方各国学者的家。有两位重要的思想家曾在这里学习。一位是金迪,他是阿拉伯著名的哲学家;另一位是数学家阿库瓦日子米,他发明了代数。

● 智慧之屋收藏并翻译了许多古老而珍贵的著作,其中包括希腊哲学家亚里士多德的作品。亚里士多德为现代科学奠定了基础。

可怕的沙尘暴

SEASON OF THE SANDSTORMS

可怕的沙尘暴

SEASON OF THE SANDSTORMS

CONTENTS

The Golden Age

Jack put his math homework aside. He opened the drawer beside his bed and pulled out a small, handmade book. For the hundredth time, he stared at the title on the cover:

> **10 MAGIC RHYMES FOR ANNIE AND JACK FROM TEDDY AND KATHLEEN**

For weeks, Jack had kept the book hidden in his drawer, wondering when he and Annie would be able to use its magi csions, and each rhyme could be used only once. Jack and Annie had already used two rhymes on a mission in Venice, Italy.

"Jack!" Annie rushed into Jack's room. Her eyes were shining. "Bring the book! Let's go!"

"Where?" said Jack.

"You know where! Come on!" Annie called as she ran

back downstairs.

Jack quickly put Teddy and Kathleen's book into his backpack. He pulled on his jacket and took off down the stairs.

Annie was waiting on the front porch. "Hurry!" she cried.

"Wait! How do you know it's there?" Jack said.

"Because I just saw it!" Annie shouted. She hurried down the porch steps and crossed the yard.

"You saw it? Actually saw it?" yelled Jack as he followed Annie through the chilly afternoon air.

"Yes! Yes!" Annie yelled.

"When?" shouted Jack.

"Just now!" said Annie. "I was walking home from the library and I had this *feeling*—so I went and looked! It's waiting for us!"

Jack and Annie raced into the Frog Creek woods. They

ran between the budding trees, over the fresh green moss of early spring, until they came to the tallest oak.

"See?" said Annie.

"Yes," breathed Jack. He stared up at the magic tree house. Its rope ladder dangled above the mossy ground. Annie started climbing up. Jack followed. When they got inside, Jack pulled off his backpack.

"Look, a book and a letter!" Annie said. She picked up a folded letter from the floor, and Jack picked up a book with a gold cover.

"Baghdad," Jack said. He showed the book to Annie. Its title was:

**THE GOLDEN AGE
OF BAGHDAD**

"A golden age?" said Annie. "That sounds cool. Let's go!"

"Wait, we should read our letter first," said Jack.

"Right," said Annie.She unfolded the paper. "Merlin's handwriting," she said. She read aloud:

> *Dear Jack and Annie of Frog Creek,*
> *Your mission is to journey to Baghdad of long ago and help the caliph spread wisdom to the world. To succeed, you must be humble and use your magic wisely. Follow these—*

"Wait, what's a *caliph?*" said Jack. "And what's Merlin mean— 'spread wisdom to the world'? That's a big responsibility."

"I don't know," said Annie. "Let me finish."She kept

reading：

> *Follow these instructions：*
> *Ride a ship of the desert*
> *on a cold starry night.*
> *Ride through the dust*
> *and hot morning light.*
>
> *Find a horse on a dome，*
> *the one who sees all，*
> *in the heart of the city*
> *behind the third wall.*
>
> *Beneath birds who sing*
> *in the Room of the Tree，*
> *greet a friend you once knew*
> *and a new friend to be.*
>
> *Remember that life*
> *is full of surprises.*
> *Return to the tree house*
> *before the moon rises.*
>
>   *—M.*

"This sounds pretty easy," said Annie.

"No, it doesn't," said Jack. "All these instructions are so mysterious. We don't know what any of them mean."

"We'll find out when we get there," said Annie. "But first we have to get there. Make the wish."

"Okay," said Jack. He pointed to the cover of the book. "I wish we could go to the golden age of Baghdad," he said.

The wind started to blow.

The tree house started to spin.

It spun faster and faster.

Then everything was still.

Absolutely still.

2

Nowhere

Jack felt hot. He opened his eyes. Burning sunlight was flooding into the tree house. He and Annie were wear ing long robes tied with cords. They wore white head cloths and pointy slip-on shoes. Jack's backpack had turned into a leather shoulder bag.

"We look like characters in that book Aunt Mary gave us," said Annie, "*Tales from the Arabian Nights.*"

"Yeah, like Aladdin and Ali Baba," said Jack.

Shading their eyes from the bright sunlight, Jack and Annie squinted out the window. They had landed in the spiky crown of a palm tree. It was the tallest tree in a clump of palm trees. Thorny shrubs and sparse green grass grew under the trees. A small spring bubbled up from the ground. Surrounding the clump of trees were miles and miles of scorching sand.

"This doesn't look like a golden age to me," said Annie.

"Yeah, and where's Baghdad?" asked Jack. He picked

up their research book and opened it to the first page. He read aloud:

> From 762 AD to 1258 AD, the Arab world had a golden age. During that time, a ruler known as a caliph (say KAY-liff) governed an empire that stretched for thousands of miles. The capital of the Arab empire was the city of Baghdad, an important center for learning and trade.

Jack looked up. "So the caliph is a ruler," he said, "and he probably lived in Baghdad."

"Yeah, but how do we *get* there?" asked Annie.

"Patience," said Jack. "Remember on our last mission,

we learned that we have to do things in order, one thing at a time." He read the first part of Merlin's instructions.

> **Ride a ship of the desert**
> **on a cold starry night.**
> **Ride through the dust**
> **and hot morning light.**

"I wonder what a 'ship of the desert' is," said Jack, looking up.

"Well, whatever it is, I'm sure we'll find it eventually," Annie said slowly, as if she were trying to sound patient. "We could just sit here and keep an eye out for a big boat. Or..."

"Or what?" said Jack.

"Maybe we could use one of Teddy and Kathleen's magic rhymes."

"Not yet," said Jack. "Merlin said to use our magic wisely. We just got here. We used two rhymes on our last mission. And we only have eight left to divide between three——"

"Okay, okay——" Annie broke in. "We can only use a rhyme when there's absolutely nothing else to do, right?"

"Right," said Jack.

"So...," said Annie. "What do *you* think we should do?"

"We could start walking," said Jack.

"Walk where?" said Annie. "Which way is Baghdad?"

Jack looked out the window. Beyond the palm trees there was nothing but sand and sky. In the distance were lonely dunes. The desert was eerily silent.

"We could, uh..." Jack couldn't think of anything else they could do. "We could look in the rhyme book," he said. Jack pulled the book of magic rhymes out of his pack. He and

Annie read down the table of contents together.

"*Make a Stone Come Alive*," read Annie. "We did that on our last mission. We can't do that again."

"It wouldn't help, anyway," said Jack. He looked at other rhymes. "*Bend Iron*," he read. "We've already done that, too."

"*Turn into Ducks*," read Annie. She looked at Jack.

"No," he said.

"*Mend What Cannot Be Mended*," read Annie.

"Nothing needs mending," said Jack.

"How about *this* one?" said Annie. "*Make Helpers Appear out of Nowhere.*"

"Well...," said Jack, "Maybe..."

"Come on, it's perfect," said Annie. "That's where we are—nowhere. And we could sure use some helpers."

"Okay," said Jack."I'll read the line Teddy wrote. You

read Kathleen's line in her selkie language."

"Okay," said Annie. She turned to the page with the rhyme. She held the book out to Jack.

Jack read in a loud, clear voice:

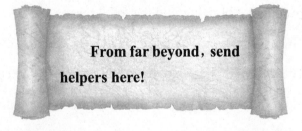

From far beyond, send helpers here!

Then Annie read:

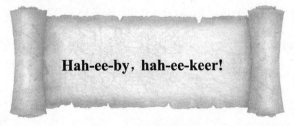

Hah-ee-by, hah-ee-keer!

The second that Annie finished the rhyme, wind gusted in from the desert, blowing a cloud of sand through the window. The wind shook the palm trees. Sand blew into Annie's

eyes. "Oww!" she said.

"Get back!" cried Jack.

Jack and Annie jumped away from the window. They pressed themselves against the wall and covered their faces. Gritty sand kept blowing into the tree house.

"It's a sandstorm!" said Jack.

The hot sand piled into drifts all over the floor. Then the wind died down as quickly as it had started. The palm trees stopped shaking.

Jack and Annie looked out the window. The air was thick with grainy dust, making it hard to see. But the sand was still.

"I think it's over," said Annie.

"I hope so," said Jack. "Why did our magic rhyme cause a sandstorm instead of sending us helpers?"

"I don't know," said Annie. "Maybe we said it wrong."

Jack brushed the sand off their research book and looked up *sandstorms* in the index. He found the right page and read:

The season of the sandstorms be-gins in the desert in mid-February and con-tinues all spring. Winds can blow as fast as 40 miles per hour. Sandstorms can easily cause travelers to lose their way in the desert.

"I don't understand," said Jack. "We don't need to lose our way. We need to *find* our way."

Just then the sound of bells came from outside.

Jack and Annie looked out the window. Through the haze，they saw four riders perched high on the humps of camels. The riders wore brightly colored robes. Behind them a dozen more camels were tied head to tail and loaded down with saddlebags. As the camels swung from side to side，bells tinkled from around their necks.

Annie grinned. "Helpers!" she said.

Mamoon

Annie stuck her head out the tree house window. "Hey!" she called.

"Shhhh!" said Jack, pulling her back in. "Don't let them see us up here! It's too hard to explain the tree house. Let's go down."

"Good point," said Annie. She handed Merlin's letter to Jack and started down the rope ladder. Jack grabbed his shoulder bag. He put the letter inside, then added their research book and rhyme book. He slung the leather bag across his chest and climbed down.

When he stepped onto the ground, Jack twisted the rope ladder behind the tree trunk so it wouldn't be noticed. "Okay," he said to Annie.

"Hey!" Annie called again, waving. She and Jack stepped out into the open.

The camel riders headed toward the palm trees. The man

in the lead made his camel kneel. As he climbed off, Jack and Annie ran over to him. The man wore a long white robe. He had a black beard and stern, dark eyes. "Who are you?" he asked, unsmiling. "From where do you come?"

"I am Annie, and this is my brother, Jack," said Annie. "Our home is far away in Frog Creek, Pennsylvania."

"I have not heard of such a place," the man said. "How do you come to be here in the desert alone?"

"Uh..." Jack didn't know what to say.

"We were riding with our family," Annie said. "We stopped to rest here. My brother and I took a nap behind these trees. When we woke up, everyone was gone. They left us by mistake. See, we have a really *big* family. There are many brothers and sisters—"

"Annie," said Jack. She was saying too much, he thought.

The man looked concerned. "Why have they not come back for you?" he said, gazing out at the desert. "I hope they

have not been attacked by bandits."

"Are there bandits around here?" asked Annie.

"There are many bandits prowling the desert," said the man.

Jack looked anxiously around at the vast sandy plain.

"That is why one must always travel with others," said the man. "But I hope your family is safe and will return for you soon."

"Excuse me," Annie said politely. "But who are you? How did you happen to come here?"

"I am a merchant," the man said. "My caravan was traveling from the west, when we were surprised by a sudden sandstorm. It seemed to come from nowhere. But luckily it brought us to this oasis. We will rest and water our animals until the sun goes down. In the cool of the night, we will travel on to Baghdad."

The caravan leader walked over to his men and spoke to them. They dismounted and started taking saddlebags off the camels.

Annie turned to Jack. "See, our rhyme worked!" she whispered. "The sandstorm was magic! It brought them here on their way to Baghdad!"

"But how can we get *them* to help us?" said Jack.

"Well, Merlin said we should be humble, so let's offer to help *them*," said Annie. She walked over to the caravan leader. He was filling a canvas bucket with water from a small spring.

"Excuse me," said Annie, "we

wondered if we could help you."

The man gave her a quick smile. "Thank you, yes, " he said. "If you could gather dates, it would be most appreciated. My men are very hungry." He handed Annie two large baskets.

"No problem, " said Annie. "We'll gather dates."

Annie carried the baskets to Jack. "Do you know what a *date* is?" she whispered. "We're supposed to gather some."

"I'll look it up, " said Jack. With his back to the camel riders, he pulled their research book out of his bag and looked

up *dates.* He read:

> **Dates are known as the fruit of the desert. They hang in bunches from date palms. People gather dates by shaking the trunk of the tree. Not only are dates an important food, but the wood and leaves of the date palm are used to make—**

"Okay, got it," interrupted Annie, putting the baskets down. "Let's start shaking the trees!"

Jack put the book away and looked around. For the first time, he noticed bunches of brown fruit hanging from the trees. He grabbed hold of the nearest tree trunk. Annie grabbed the trunk from the other side. Together they shook the tree un-

til dates began falling to the ground.

In the desert heat, Jack and Annie went from tree to tree, shaking each one and gathering the dates that fell to the ground. By the time they had filled their baskets, the trees were casting long shadows over the oasis.

Tired and sweaty, Jack and Annie carried their heavy baskets back to the caravan leader. He was boiling water over a fire of twigs. "Ah, very good," he said. "Thank you, Jack and Annie."

"You're welcome," said Annie. "What else can we do for you?"

"Yor should rest from the heat now," said the man. "Would you like to sit and have tea with us?"

"Sure," said Annie. "By the way, what's your name?"

"My name is very long," the man said with a smile. "You may call me Mamoon."

While their camels grazed, Mamoon and his men sat on a woolen rug spread over the grass. They shared dates and tea with Jack and Annie. The dark, plump fruit was sweet and chewy. The tea was strong but good.

In the fiery red glow of the setting sun, Jack watched the grazing camels. He thought the humped animals looked really funny. They had knobby knees, big clumsy feet, and little ears that twitched. Some camels smacked their droopy lips as they drank water. Others gobbled down whole branches of thornbushes without chewing.

"Don't the thorns hurt the camels' throats?" Jack asked Mamoon.

"No," said the caravan leader, "Their mouths are very

tough. They can eat anything: sticks, bones——"

"Even our tents and saddlebags if wc let them!" said a young camel rider.

Annie and Jack laughed. "What's in your saddlebags?" Annie asked.

"Our bags are filled with goods from Greece, Turkey, and Syria," said Mamoon. "We have many things: jewels, beads, and precious spices, such as cinnamon, pepper, and vanilla. We are taking everything to Baghdad to sell."

"We have to get to Baghdad, too," said Annie. "We have to meet with the caliph."

The camel riders chuckled as if they thought Annie was making a joke.

Only Mamoon did not laugh. "Your family is to meet with the caliph?" he said.

"No," said Annie. "Just Jack and me. We have to help

him spread wisdom to the world."

"*Annie*," warned Jack.

The camel riders laughed loudly.

"What's so funny?" Annie asked.

"The caliph does not meet with children," said a young man. "He is the most powerful and important person in the world."

"Oh," said Annie, frowning.

The news worried Jack, too.

Mamoon looked at Annie and Jack with a curious expression. "Night will soon be upon us. Since your family has not yet returned, would you like to travel with us to Baghdad?" he said. "You have journeyed by camel this far. I trust you can ride camels the rest of the way."

"Sure we can!" said Annie. "We *love* camels!"

We do? thought Jack.

"Good. We love our ships of the desert, too," said Ma-moon. "We will set sail on them soon."

"So that's what 'ships of the desert' are!" Annie whispered to Jack.

Camels, thought Jack. *Oh, brother.*

Ships of the Desert

The camel riders all silently watched the sun set over the faraway dunes. As the fiery ball slipped beneath the horizon, the desert was flooded with red light. As soon as the sun disappeared, the air grew much cooler.

Mamoon stood up. "It is time to go," he said.

The camel riders put out their small fire. In the growing darkness, Mamoon helped them saddle up their animals and load them with baggage.

Then Mamoon came over to Jack and Annie. "You can ride those two sisters," he said, pointing to two camels kneeling in the sand. "Climb on, then come to the front of the line to ride with me."

Jack and Annie walked over to the two camel sisters. Each had reins hanging from her neck. Saddles made from colorful cushions were piled high on their humps.

Annie patted the wiry, tan-colored fur of one of the cam-

els. The camel looked at Annie with big eyes and fluttered her thick eyelashes. "Hey, Cutie," said Annie.

The other camel nuzzled Annie's neck. "Hey, Beauty," Annie said to the other. "You want some attention, too?"

"*Cutie* and *Beauty*?" said Jack. He didn't find either camel particularly cute or beautiful.

Annie climbed onto Cutie's saddle cushion and picked up the reins. "Let's ride!" she said.

Cutie rose awkwardly up from a kneeling position to a full stand. "Oh, wow!" said Annie, towering over Jack. "She's really tall."

Jack started to climb onto Beauty. But the camel caught an end of his head cloth and began chewing it.

"Stop that!" said Jack, pulling the cloth away from her. Beauty opened her mouth wide and flashed rows of sharp teeth. Jack drew back.

"Don't be afraid," said Annie.

"Easy for *you* to say," said Jack. "Yours likes you."

"Don't worry, Beauty likes you, too," said Annie. "I can tell." Annie's camel began ambling toward the other camels waiting to head off into the desert. "Come on, Jack! It's really fun once you're moving!" she called.

"Fun," muttered Jack, "Right." He held on to the ends of his head cloth and put his leg over Beauty's hump. The camel eyed him suspiciously. She swished her tail, slapping his back.

"Hey!" said Jack.

Jack tried to get comfortable on the saddle cushion.But Beauty spat at him and made a weird screeching sound.

"Quiet!" said Jack. He hooked his shoulder bag onto a saddle horn. When he was finally settled, Beauty turned her head and started chewing on his leather bag.

"No! Don't!" yelled Jack. He tried pulling the bag away, but Beauty played tug-of-war. "Come on, let go," Jack said. "Give it back, stupid!"

"Do you really think she is stupid?"

Jack jumped. Mamoon had ridden up behind him and was watching as he tried to get his bag back from Beauty.

Jack was embarrassed. "Um, she won't let go of my stuff," he said.

Mamoon grabbed the strap of Jack's bag. He clucked his

tongue, and the camel let go. She groaned as Mamoon hooked the leather bag back onto the saddle horn.

"For thousands of years, camels like this one have carried people across the desert," said Mamoon. "She is truly a miracle of nature."

Some miracle, thought Jack.

"She can drink two barrels of water in ten minutes," said Mamoon, "and then go for a week without drinking again.

She can live many days without food, too."

"Really?" said Jack.

"She is well suited to travel in the desert," said Mamoon. "Her thick eyebrows protect her eyes from the glare of the sun. Her long eyelashes and the fur

around her ears keep out the windblown sand."

"Cool," said Jack softly.

"Her feet are so tough, they do not feel the heat of the desert," said Mamoon. "And they are so big that they keep her from sinking down into the loose sand."

"Hmm," said Jack.

"She can carry five hundred pounds of baggage on her back,"said Mamoon, "and travel one hundred miles in a single day."

"That's a lot," murmured Jack.

Mamoon tugged on the camel's reins and clucked his tongue. Beauty breathed heavily as she rose up on her long, powerful legs to her full height.

Mamoon looked at Jack. "We must respect her and honor her," he said. "In many ways, she is superior to us, no?"

Jack nodded. He thought of the words of Merlin's letter.

To succeed in your mission, you must be humble. He patted the camel. "Good girl, Beauty."

Mamoon clucked his tongue again to coax the camel forward. Perched high on his saddle, Jack rocked from side to side. He did not feel at all safe, but he stayed calm. Beauty ambled over to Cutie. The two sisters stood together and snorted.

The desert sky was bright with stars. Mamoon called to his men, and the caravan started moving forward.

The camels walked with a swaying motion. They moved two big feet on one side, then two big feet on the other. Jack gripped the horn of his saddle as his "ship of the desert" rocked from left to right.

"Isn't this fun?" said Annie, rocking alongside him.

"Sort of," said Jack, shivering. Actually, he wasn't having any fun at all. He felt seasick and was freezing in

the night air. Also，he was worried about their mission. Would the caliph meet with them? If he did，how could they help him "spread wisdom to the world"? And if Baghdad was very far away，how would they ever find their way back to the tree house?

Mamoon slowed his camel until he was riding between Jack and Annie. "When I was a boy，I spent many cold nights in the desert riding with my father on journeys to the west，" he said. "At first，I，too，thought camels were foolish. I always longed for more blankets and for a smoother ride. I wished to be back in Baghdad in my own warm bed."

Jack smiled. He liked the caravan leader.

"But over time, I have come to love the cold desert nights,"
said Mamoon. "Now when I am sleeping in my warm bed in
Baghdad, I long to be here instead. I wish to be reading the wind
and the stars."

"How do you read the stars?" asked Annie.

"They have their own language,"said Mamoon. "At
this moment, we are heading east, toward the Goat Star." he
pointed at the sky.

Jack couldn't tell which star was the Goat Star. But he
was filled with wonder. Thousands of tiny lights twinkled in
the black dome of night. There were more stars than Jack had
ever imagined. Some looked close enough to touch.

Mamoon started singing a song. The other camel riders
joined in. Jack couldn't understand the words, but the tune
was soothing. The camels seemed to sway to the music.

Jack stopped worrying about how they would get back to

the tree house. And he found he was actually enjoying the fresh desert air. He started to relax.

"Jack," Annie said softly. "Guess what—we just solved the first mystery in Merlin's letter: *Ride a ship of the desert on a cold starry night.*"

"Yeah," said Jack happily. "And it's really fun."

Suddenly a fierce shout came from the distance. Jack sat up straighter. His heart thumped.

"Bandits!" one of the camel drivers shouted.

Bandits!

Jack looked around wildly. Dark figures on horses were galloping across the sand toward them. They were yelling and shouting.

"Oh, no!" cried Jack. "What should we do?"

"We will fight them off!" said Mamoon. "You and Annie take this box and ride to the dunes!" Mamoon pulled a flat wooden box out of one of his saddlebags. He thrust the box into Jack's hands. "Hurry! Ride as fast as you can! Protect it with your lives!"

Jack frantically tried to stuff the box into his shoulder bag. But Mamoon slapped the back of Jack's camel, and she bolted forward. The reins slipped from Jack's hands. He grabbed the saddle horn with one hand and clutched the wooden box to his chest with the other. He held on for his life as Beauty galloped across the dark desert.

Annie's camel ran beside Jack's. Like two racehorses,

Beauty and Cutie thundered across the sand toward the distant dunes. Rocking crazily from side to side, Jack clung to the box. "Slow down!" he yelled. "Please!"

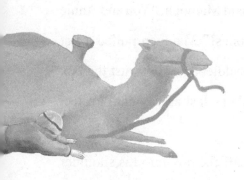

It was no use. Beauty ran like the wind. She and her sister practically flew over the desert under the starry sky. Jack wanted the camels to stop. But at the same time, he wanted to get far away from the bandits.

Finally the camels began to slow their pace. Jack looked back. He couldn't see the caravan at all, and no one seemed to be following them.

When the two camels reached the dunes, they began plodding around the steep hills. Once they were nestled safely

between tall sand drifts, they stopped to rest. Beauty grunted.
Cutie snorted.

"Thanks...thanks, girls," said Annie, panting.

"I hope Mamoon and the others are safe from the bandits," said Jack.

"Me too," said Annie. "What's
in the box he gave us?"

Jack held up the flat wooden
box. "I don't know," he said. "But
Mamoon said we should protect it
with our lives."

"Maybe it's a precious spice," said Annie.

"I hope it's more than *that*,"said Jack. "I'd hate to risk
my life for cinnamon or pepper."

"Should we look?" said Annie.

"I don't know," said Jack. "Mamoon might not want

us to."

"But don't you think we could protect it better if we knew what it was?" said Annie.

"Maybe...," said Jack. He could see Annie's point. "Okay."

Jack tried to open the lid of the box, but he couldn't. In the dark, his finger pressed against a keyhole. "Forget it," he said. "It's locked."

"Shh! Listen!" said Annie.

Jack listened. He heard a high-pitched moaning sound. It sounded like music from a violin. Wafting through the dry sand dunes, the haunting music grew louder.

"What *is* that?" said Jack.

"Uh-oh," said Annie. "Now I hear something else."

Jack held his breath. He heard hooves galloping over the desert. "The bandits!" he said.

"We have to hide the box!" said Annie.

"Where?" said Jack.

"In the sand!" said Annie. She clucked her tongue, and Cutie knelt down to the ground. Beauty knelt, too. Jack and Annie jumped off their saddle cushions and started digging in the sand.

The sound of hoofbeats grew louder and louder. Jack and Annie dug frantically. They threw sand behind them like puppies digging in the dirt.

"That's deep enough!" said Jack. He placed the box in the hole they had dug. Then he and Annie pushed piles of sand back on top of it.

When they stood up, Annie gasped. "Look!"

A dark figure on a camel was silhouetted against the starlit sky. The rider was winding his way through the dunes toward them. Jack's heart nearly pounded out of his chest.

"Should we use a magic rhyme?" Annie asked.

"We don't have time!" said Jack.

The rider drew closer, until he stopped in front of Jack and Annie. "You are safe, no?" he said.

"Mamoon!" said Annie.

Relief flooded through Jack. He laughed. "Yes, we're safe!" he said. "And *you're* safe, too!"

"My men fought well," said Mamoon. "The thieves fled with only a few bags of pepper and painted beads."

"And we kept your box safe, too!" said Annie proudly. She knelt and dug in the sand until she uncovered the wooden box. She handed it to Mamoon.

"Ahh, very good," the caravan leader said.

"What's in the box?" asked Annie.

"A priceless treasure," said Mamoon. "I have brought it all the way from Greece. And I am taking it to Baghdad. Thank you both for guarding it with your lives. You are

very special."

"Sure, no problem," said Jack. He still wondered what was in the box. *Gold? Silver? Precious jewels?*

But Mamoon did not say. He put the box back into his camel's saddlebag. "Let us be on our way now," he said.

Jack climbed on top of his kneeling camel. He clucked his tongue. He was surprised and pleased when Beauty rose up on her tall legs.

"We will catch up with the others in Baghdad," said Mamoon. "If all goes well, we will arrive in the city in the afternoon. We must head east toward the morning sun."

Mamoon rode out of the dunes. Jack and Annie followed him. As their camels rocked through the chilly dawn, daylight shimmered over the sand.

"Mamoon, last night we heard strange sounds in the dunes," said Annie. "Like music playing."

神奇树屋
MAGIC TREE HOUSE

"Ah, yes," said Mamoon, "*the whistling sands*."

"What are the whistling sands?" asked Jack.

"Some say it is magic," said Mamoon. "But I believe that all things in nature have their reasons. That is why I like the study of *science*. Science says we must observe our world. We must make experiments and try to find out why things happen. We have learned the whistling is made by sands settling in the drifts."

"Oh," said Annie. "I'd hoped it was magic."

"Learning the reasons for things *is* magic," said Mamoon. "True knowledge brings light to the world. And that is a magical thing, no?"

"Yes," said Jack.

Annie nodded thoughtfully. "I guess, when you put it that way," she said.

Swaying from side to side on their camels, the three rid-

可怕的沙尘暴

Season
of the
Sandstorms

ers traveled toward the dawn. As the sun rose higher in the sky, the desert grew blazing hot. A dry wind whipped through the air, making snaky patterns in the sand.

Mamoon halted his camel. He looked around and frowned.

"What's wrong?" said Jack. "Are there signs of bandits?"

Mamoon shook his head. "No, it is the desert itself that worries me now," he said. "It is restless." He clucked his tongue, and his camel began walking again.

As they rode over the restless desert, the wind picked up loose sand and tossed it into the air. Jack and Annie lowered their heads to keep the sand from blowing into their eyes. Their head cloths flapped in the wind. More and more sand started blowing. The desert seemed alive as the sand shifted and swirled.

Mamoon stopped again and looked about. The snaky patterns in the sand were blowing into round, curly patterns. Jack heard a weird moaning sound. "Is that the whistling sands again?" he asked hopefully.

"No," said Mamoon. "That is the cry of a terrible sandstorm. And it will soon be upon us."

6

Sandblasted

In the distance, a haze of sand was spreading over the desert. As the wind picked up, the sky turned red and the haze thickened into a brown cloud. The cloud began gliding toward Jack, Annie, and Mamoon like a moving wall.

"Get down! Lie on your bellies!" ordered Mamoon. "Quickly! Cover your faces with your head cloths!"

Jack clucked his tongue. Beauty knelt to the ground. Jack, Annie, and Mamoon jumped off their camels and lay down on the sand beside them.

Jack tried desperately to cover his face with his head cloth, but the raging wind kept whipping the cloth from his hands. The sky turned from red to black. The moaning sound turned into a loud rumbling.

Jack looked up and saw the wind rip the saddlebag off Mamoon's kneeling camel! The bag hit the ground and fell open. The box bounced out and tumbled away in the driving

wind.

"The treasure!" cried Jack, but his voice was drowned out by the wind. He jumped up and bolted after the box.

Jack raced across the desert as the sand battered his body. The wind tried to push him down. But Jack ran with all his might, until finally he caught up with the box and threw himself down on top of it. He grabbed the ends of his head scarf and covered his face.

The sandstorm blasted over Jack, sounding like the hoofbeats of a hundred galloping camels. Jack's eyes burned. He felt as if he were suffocating.

Slowly the thundering softened to a low rumbling. The rumbling faded to a moaning. The wind died down. The hot desert grew still and silent.

Coughing, Jack rolled over and sat up. He had sand in his mouth, sand in his ears, and sand in his nose. He pulled

off his glasses and rubbed his stinging eyes. But rubbing only made them worse.

Blinking, Jack clutched the box and looked around for the others. The air was thick with dust. He had completely lost his sense of direction.

"Jack! Jack!" He heard Annie shouting.

Jack clutched the small wooden box and stood up. His legs were so wobbly, he fell over. "Annie!" he croaked.

"Jack!" she called through the dust. "Where are you?"

"Here!" he said.

"Where?"

"Here!"

"*There* you are!" said Annie, stumbling out of the haze. "Are you okay?"

"I'm okay," croaked Jack. "Are you?"

"Yes! I ran after you," said Annie. Her voice was ho-

arse, too.

"I had to save the box," said Jack. "Where's Mamoon?"

"I don't know," said Annie. "I don't think he saw us chase after the box."

"Mamoon!" they shouted together. "Mamoon!"

There was no answer.

Peering through the sandy haze, Jack heard thumping sounds. He and Annie turned around. Their two camels were trotting toward them.

"Cutie!" cried Annie. "Beauty!"

Jack and Annie stumbled to their camels and grabbed their reins.

"Thank you for finding us!" said Annie.

"Yeah, thanks," said Jack, patting Beauty.

"Mamoon!" Annie called. "Mamoon!"

"He must have gone in the wrong direction to look for

us, " said Jack.

"If we don't find him, how will we get to Baghdad? And what will we do with his treasure?" asked Annie.

"I don't know, " said Jack. He held up the wooden box.

"Look, the top's broken, " said Annie. She pointed to a long crack running down the lid of the box.

"I hope the treasure wasn't hurt, " said Jack.

"Maybe we should check and see, "said Annie.

Jack took a deep breath. He still thought Mamoon might not want them to look inside the box. But his curiosity got the best of him. "Okay, " he said. "I guess it wouldn't hurt to make sure it's all right."

Jack pried apart the two pieces of wood and lifted them off. Inside the box was a book.

"A book?" said Jack, surprised. He'd expected gold or jewels. He carefully lifted the book out of the box. It had a

plain leather cover with no title on it.

"It doesn't *look* like a precious treasure," said Annie.

"Maybe the writing inside is the treasure," said Jack.

Jack gently opened the book. Inside were pages of thick yellow paper. The pages were bound with stitching and covered with writing on both sides. The first page said:

**THE WRITINGS OF
ARISTOTLE**

"Who is Ar-is-totle?" said Annie, sounding out the name.

"I don't know," said Jack. "I'll look him up in our research book." He unhooked his bag from the saddle horn. Sand covered the books inside. He pulled out their research

book and brushed it off. Then he looked up *Aristotle* in the index. "Good. He's here," Jack said. He turned to the right page and read:

> **Aristotle (say AIR-is-TAH-tul) lived in ancient Greece over 2,300 years ago. He is known as one of the greatest *philosophers* of all time. The word philosopher means "lover of wisdom." Aristotle's works were introduced to the Western world by the Arabs in the Middle Ages.**

"So Aristotle was a great lover of wisdom," said Annie.

"I guess so," said Jack. "But I wonder why this book is such a treasure."

"Wait a minute," said Annie. "Doesn't Merlin's note tell us that we have to help the caliph of Baghdad spread *wisdom* to the world?"

Jack caught his breath. "Yeah," he said. "And if this is a book of Aristotle's writings, it must be full of wisdom... We have to get this book to the caliph—that's our mission for Merlin!"

"We better get going!" said Annie.

Jack and Annie pulled on the reins of their camels and clucked their tongues. Beauty and Cutie knelt in the sand, and Jack and Annie climbed on. Leaving the broken box behind, Jack carefully packed the ancient book of Aristotle's wisdom and the research book into his bag. Then he hung the bag from his saddle horn.

"Which way?" said Annie.

"Toward the rising sun in the east," said Jack. "That's

what Mamoon said."

"It's that way, then," said Annie. She pointed toward a bright blur in the hazy sky.

Jack and Annie's camels headed into the dusty, glaring sun. "Hey, we're following Merlin's second instruction now," said Annie. *"Ride through the dust and hot morning light."*

"You're right," said Jack.

As Jack and Annie kept traveling toward the east, the desert sands shimmered and sparkled with heat. The air cleared, but still they saw no sign of Mamoon.

Jack looked down to shield his eyes from the burning sunlight. Exhausted, he closed his eyes. As Beauty swayed gently from side to side, Jack's head dropped forward. Suddenly he heard Annie shout, "Jack! Look!"

"What? Mamoon?"said Jack, jerking awake.

"No! Look!" said Annie.

In the distance，Jack saw sunlit towers and domes shining against the clear blue sky. "Oh，man，" he whispered. *"Baghdad."*

Behind the Third Wall

"Let's hurry!" said Annie.

As Beauty and Cutie walked toward Baghdad, the loose sand of the desert changed to sunbaked earth. Then the hard earth changed to scrubby grass. Goats and sheep grazed in the grass, and farms dotted the countryside.

It wasn't long before Jack and Annie came to a red clay path. The path led to a crossroads where many travelers were coming from different directions. They were all heading toward the shining city. Jack and Annie rode alongside boys driving sheep and farmers in donkey carts. They passed women with veils over their faces, carrying pots on their shoulders.

Jack kept looking for Mamoon. But he never saw him. Moving with the crowd, Beauty and Cutie clomped across a bridge. Rowboats and barges glided along the yellowish brown river.

On the other side of the river was a huge outdoor market with a maze of tents. The market seemed to be filled with people from many countries. The sharp smell of incense filled the air. Stalls were jammed with burlap sacks, baskets, and carpets. Shoemakers sat cross-legged, stitching shoes. Potters were bent over ovens, baking earth-colored pots. Weavers sat at small looms, spinning silk brocade.

"Paper? Pearls?" a merchant shouted.

"No thanks!" said Annie.

"Pigeons, parrots?" another shouted at Jack.

"No thanks!" he said.

"I love this place!" said Annie. "What is it?"

"I'll look it up," said Jack. He pulled out their research

book and read:

> In the ninth century, traders from all over the world brought their goods to Baghdad to sell. Baghdad merchants traded paper, fine cloth, and jewelry for goods from Spain, India, Africa, China, Greece, and other lands. These goods were sold in a huge open-air market called a bazaar.

"Oh, so a *bazaar* is sort of like a mall," said Jack.

"It's a lot *better* than a mall!" said Annie. "Let's get off and look around."

"We don't have time to shop," said Jack. "We have to finish our mission." He pulled out Merlin's letter and read:

Find a horse on a dome，
the one who sees all，
in the heart of the city
behind the third wall.

"It sounds like we pass three walls and then we come to a horse，" said Jack. "We'd better keep going."

Jack put the book and letter away. Beauty and Cutie ambled through the noisy bazaar. When they left the bazaar，they came to a curved brick wall. Running along the base of the wall was a muddy moat.

"Look—that must be the first wall!" said Annie.

"Cool，" said Jack.

Jack and Annie rode the two camels over an arched bridge that crossed the moat. They passed through a gate with

double iron doors. On the other side of the wall was a busy avenue lined with buildings.

As their camels wove slowly in and out of the crowd, Jack pulled out their research book. Swaying from side to side, he read to Annie:

> During its golden age, Baghdad had good hospitals. The city was also known for its excellent police system and public schools, along with its many libraries and stores and a zoo with a hundred lions.

"I'd like to visit those lions," said Annie.

"We don't have time now," said Jack.

Their camels clopped down the busy avenue until they

came to a green field.

"Look, there's the second wall!" said Annie.

Bordering the field was another wall. It was curved, too, but much taller than the first. It looked like it was at least a hundred feet high. There were guards at the gate, but they didn't seem to be checking any of the people passing through.

"Act normal," Jack advised Annie. "Don't attract their attention."

Jack and Annie joined a stream of people passing through the gate. Beyond the second wall was another grand avenue. And at the end of the wide cobbled road was another green field. "Look! The third wall!" said Annie.

The third wall was even taller than the second. Again, people were passing freely through its gate.

"This part of the mission is easy!" said Annie.

"Yeah," said Jack. "But we still have to find that horse

on the dome, and then find the caliph and get him to meet
with us."

Beauty and Cutie ambled through the gate of the third
wall, carrying Jack and Annie into the heart of Baghdad. A
palace loomed before them. Its roof was a glittering green
dome. At the top of the dome stood the statue of a horse.

"Yay, the horse who sees all!" said Annie. "I'll bet the
caliph lives in that palace. Let's follow those people inside."
She pointed to a stream of people entering an arched passage-
way outside the palace.

Jack and Annie rode under
the arch and into a beautiful gar-
den. The warm breeze smelled of
flowers. They rode down a path

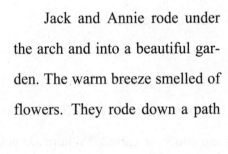

bordered by date palms until they came to a courtyard where boys were playing ball. Near the courtyard was a stable with camels in it.

"Looks like we'll have to go the rest of the way on foot," said Jack.

"Yeah, I guess Beauty and Cutie can stay there," said Annie, pointing to the stable.

Jack and Annie rode into the stable. They clucked, and the camels knelt. As Jack reached for his shoulder bag, a ball rolled into the stable. Annie picked it up and stepped outside. Jack followed her.

"Here!" shouted a young boy with curly black hair. He was holding out his hands. Annie threw the ball to him, and the boy caught it. He grinned at Annie's good throw. "Who are you?" he called. "Where are you from?"

Before Jack could say anything, Annie crossed to the

boys. Jack hurried after her.

"I'm Annie and this is my brother, Jack," Annie said. "We're from Frog Creek, Pennsylvania."

"Why have you come to Baghdad?" the boy asked.

"We have to see the caliph," said Annie.

The boy and his friends laughed.

"What's so funny?" said Annie.

"Our caliph is the most powerful man in the world," said another boy. "He does not have time to visit with children."

"That's what everyone keeps saying," said Annie. "But we're here on a very important mission. We——"

"Annie," Jack interrupted, "come on. I left my bag back in the stable." He waved to the boys. "See you guys later. Let's go, Annie."

Annie started to leave with Jack.

"When you discover that the caliph will not meet with

you, come back and play with us," called the curly-haired boy.

Annie stopped. "Don't worry," she called back. "He'll meet with us! We're special!"

"Annie, come on," said Jack.

"Why are *you* special?" shouted the boy.

"For one thing, we just saved a precious treasure from bandits and from a sandstorm in the desert," said Annie. "For another—"

"Annie!" Jack said sternly. He grabbed her arm. "Come *on*!" He pulled Annie away.

As they headed back into the stable, Jack shook his head. "Don't say stuff like that," he said.

"Why not?" said Annie.

"Because it's bragging," said Jack. "It makes other kids feel bad. Even if you *are* special, you don't have to—"

"Oh, no!" cried Annie. She covered her mouth with her hands.

"What?" said Jack, following her shocked gaze.

Jack's leather bag lay at Beauty's feet. It was open. Beside it was the torn leather cover of Aristotle's book. Wet pages hung in shreds from Beauty's mouth as she happily chewed the precious treasure.

Room of the Tree

"Nooooo!" cried Jack.

Jack ran to Beauty and yanked hunks of paper from her mouth. Annie dropped to her knees and picked up the torn pieces strewn around the camel's big feet.

"The treasure's ruined!" moaned Annie.

Jack was stunned. "I shouldn't have left my bag here," he said.

"No, it's all my fault. I shouldn't have gone back and bragged to those kids," wailed Annie. "I should have acted more humble, like Merlin said." Annie sounded like she was about to cry.

"It's okay," said Jack. But he knew it wasn't. The book was destroyed. They'd failed in their mission.

"Maybe—maybe we can fix it," said Annie.

Jack shook his head. "No, we can't," he said. "It's completely destroyed. It can't be fixed."

Annie looked up. "What—what did you just say?" she said.

"I said it can't be fixed," said Jack.

A big grin crossed Annie's face. "Right! It can't be fixed!" she said. "Help me gather up all these pieces!"

"Why?" said Jack. Had Annie gone nuts?

"Just do it! Quick!" said Annie.

Jack and Annie rushed around the stable, gathering up all the torn pages.

"Now pile everything over here on top of the cover and give me the book," said Annie.

"What book?" said Jack.

"The rhyme book!" said Annie.

"Oh. Oh!" said Jack. "Right!" He reached into his shoulder bag and pulled out Teddy and Kathleen's book of magic rhymes.

Jack opened the book and read down the list. "Here it is: *Mend What Cannot Be Mended*," he said.

"That's the one," said Annie.

Jack flipped through the pages until he came to the rhyme. He held up the book so he and Annie could both see. Standing in a shaft of sunlight, Jack read in a loud, clear voice:

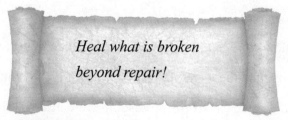

*Heal what is broken
beyond repair!*

Annie read the second line:

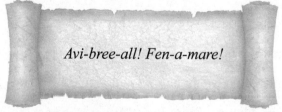

Avi-bree-all! Fen-a-mare!

The paper bits fluttered. They began to swirl off the floor.

They swirled up and around as if they were caught in a small tornado. The tornado captured all the torn pieces in its funnel and twisted them together. The papers swirled into a blur of blinding light.

Jack shielded his eyes. He heard a loud *whoof*! When he looked up, the bright tornado had vanished.

Lying on the floor of the stable in front of Jack and Annie was the ancient book.

Holding his breath, Jack carefully picked up the treasure. He opened the leather cover. "Oh, man," he whispered. Aristotle's priceless words of wisdom were neatly written on the yellow pages. There was no sign of a rip or tear anywhere.

"Thank goodness," breathed Annie.

"Yeah," said Jack.

"So what do we do now?" said Annie.

"I don't know," said Jack. "What's the next thing Mer-

lin tells us to do?" He pulled out Merlin's letter and read:

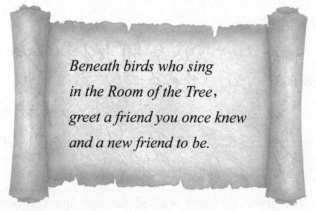

Beneath birds who sing
in the Room of the Tree,
greet a friend you once knew
and a new friend to be.

"What's that mean?" said Jack.

Suddenly Jack heard someone behind them. He and Annie turned around. A girl was standing in the doorway of the stable. She wore a long white gown. Her hair and face were hidden by a veil.

"Hi," said Annie. "Who are you?"

"I am a servant of the palace," the girl whispered. "Come."

She motioned for them to follow her.

"Let's go," Annie said to Jack.

"Where is she taking us?" asked Jack. "And why is she whispering?"

"I don't know," said Annie. "But I feel like we should follow her."

"Okay," said Jack. He put the book of wisdom and the book of magic rhymes into his bag. He slung the bag over his shoulder and followed Annie and the servant girl out of the stable.

The three of them walked through the courtyard and through the palace doors. They walked down a wide candlelit hallway over a thick woven carpet.

At the end of the hallway was a tall, carved door. A boy servant stood by the door. He wore baggy trousers and a long shirt. His face was almost completely hidden by his head cloth. He did not speak or look at them.

The servant girl stood close to Jack and Annie. In her strange, whispery voice, she said, "In front of the chair, bow to the floor.

Do not look up and do not speak until you are spoken to."

"But what— " said Jack.

"Go quickly," whispered the girl.

The boy servant pulled open the heavy door. The girl servant pushed them into the room.

"Wait," said Jack.

But the boy servant closed the door behind them, leaving Jack and Annie alone.

"Jack, look! We're here!" said Annie. "The Room of the Tree!"

Jack turned around. A giant tree stood in the center of the room. It had silver leaves that fluttered as if blown by the wind. Mechanical golden birds sang *"Tweet-tweet!"* from the silver branches.

Beneath the strange tree was an empty black chair. Jewels sparkled in its shiny wood.

"We're in the right place," said Annie. She quoted from Merlin's letter:

*Beneath birds who sing
in the Room of the Tree,
greet a friend you once knew
and a new friend to be.*

"Another mystery solved," Annie said.

"Not really," said Jack. "Where are the two friends?"

"I don't know, but we better bow in front of the chair like that servant girl told us to," said Annie.

Jack and Annie knelt in front of the shiny black chair. They bowed their heads to the floor. Jack gripped his bag with the treasure inside.

"Remember what else she said," Annie reminded Jack.

"Don't look up and don't speak until we're spoken to."

"But there's no one here," said Jack. He felt foolish, bowing in front of a chair and listening to the chirping of mechanical birds. *Why are we doing this*? he wondered.

The door opened with a low creaking sound. Jack squeezed his eyes shut. He heard footsteps moving past them.

"How did you get into the throne room?" a deep, gruff voice asked.

"A servant brought us here," said Annie.

"And why have you come?" asked the voice.

"We have a priceless treasure to give to the caliph of Baghdad," said Jack, keeping his head down. "It's a book of wisdom."

Jack fumbled in his bag and pulled out the book. He kept his eyes tightly shut as he held the book up toward the voice.

There was a long silence.

"We hope it will help the caliph spread wisdom to the world," said Annie.

"How did you come to be in possession of this book?" the man asked.

"We were helping a friend," said Annie. "And we got separated in a sandstorm."

"Ah, then I suppose you brought this book to Baghdad to gain a reward," said the man.

"No! No, we didn't," said Jack. "It was our mission to give it to the caliph."

"Surely you must be seeking some payment in exchange for this treasure," said the man. "Would you not like precious perfumes gathered from the sweetest flowers on earth?"

"No thank you," said Annie.

"Rubies as large as hens' eggs?" said the man.

"No thanks," said Jack.

"You would not accept the book's weight in gold?" said the man.

"We don't need a reward, really," said Jack.

"Since he likes books so much, why don't you just tell the caliph to use his gold and rubies to buy more of them?" said Annie.

Again, there was silence. Then the man cleared his throat. When he spoke, his voice was gentle and familiar-sounding. "Look up at me, Jack and Annie," he said.

Jack opened his eyes. He slowly lifted his head. First he saw gleaming gold slippers...then a long white robe with gold trim... then a familiar face.

Jack gasped. He couldn't believe his eyes. The man wasn't a scary person at all. The man was Mamoon!

House of Wisdom

可怕的沙尘暴
Season
of the
Sandstorms

"Mamoon?" said Annie.

"Yes," said Mamoon. "I am very glad to see that you have safely arrived in Baghdad."

"We're glad you're safe, too!" said Annie. "We were worried about you."

"I looked everywhere for you after the sandstorm," said Mamoon. "Finally I gave up my search and returned sadly to Baghdad. I assume you found your family?"

"Uh, sure," said Annie, "we found them."

"And we found your book," said Jack. "When we couldn't find you, we decided that we should give the book to the caliph."

Mamoon smiled. "You still do not understand, do you?" he said.

"Understand what?" said Annie.

"I am Caliph Abdullah al-Mamoon."

"*You're* the caliph?" said Annie.

"But—how—what?" stammered Jack.

"For many years, I have wanted a book of Aristotle's wisdom," explained the caliph. "I heard that such a book had been found in the city of Damascus, and I made arrangements to acquire it for my library. It was most important that it arrive here safely. I have long wished to travel again through the desert as I did when I was a boy. So I disguised myself as a humble merchant and made the journey. My fellow travelers never knew my true identity."

"Wow," whispered Jack.

"You have shown me that you have a great respect for books and learning," said Caliph al-Mamoon. "And you have also proven you have humble hearts. Before you join your family, I want to show you a very special place. I call it the House of Wisdom."

"*The House of Wisdom?*" breathed Jack. "That sounds

great."

"It is my hope that the world will indeed find it 'great,' "
said the caliph. "Come." He started to leave the room. Jack
and Annie rose from the floor and hurried after him.

Carrying the ancient book of Aristotle, the caliph led
Jack and Annie out of the Room of the Tree. His gold-trimmed
robe billowed about him as he swept down the corridor. Every
person he passed bowed low to the floor.

"Another mystery solved!" Annie said to Jack. She quoted from Merlin's letter:

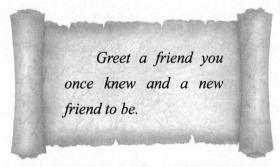

*Greet a friend you
once knew and a new
friend to be.*

"Both friends are the same person!" said Annie. "Ma-

moon from the desert and Caliph Abdullah al-Mamoon."

"Right," said Jack, smiling.

The caliph led Jack and Annie out the front doors of the palace. In the courtyard stood two camels with long poles attached to their saddles. Resting on top of the poles was a small carriage decorated with gold tassels and brass bells.

Servants helped Jack, Annie, and Caliph Abdullah al-Mamoon into the strange little carriage. Bells jingled as the camels began to move slowly through the courtyard.

The caliph opened tiny shutters to let in air and sunlight. Jack looked out. Everyone bowed as the royal carriage passed by: the boys playing ball, the gardeners weeding flower beds, the women carrying pots.

Jack had lots of questions about the House of Wisdom. But now that he knew their friend Mamoon was the mighty caliph, he felt shy. Even Annie seemed to be at a loss for words as they

rode past the date palms and the palace gardens.

"We are here," said the caliph as the camels came to a stop. He helped Jack and Annie out of the carriage. Then he led them up the steps of a large brick building.

"Welcome to the House of Wisdom," said the caliph, "a learning center for the entire world."

"What happens here?" asked Jack.

"Come, I will show you." The caliph escorted Jack and Annie through the front door and down a wide hallway. "We have a laboratory for discovering new medicines," he said, "and an observatory for viewing the stars and planets. But *this* is my favorite room of all."

The caliph stopped before an arched doorway. He opened the door and led Jack and Annie into a huge, silent room. "This is the library," he said in a hushed voice. "Even I must be very quiet here."

神奇 树 屋
MAGIC TREE HOUSE

Late-afternoon light slanted down from high, open windows, streaming over bookshelves and colorful carpets. Men read at long tables. When the readers looked up and saw the caliph, they all started to rise.

"Please continue with your work. Do not mind us," the caliph said softly.

The men sat down again and returned to their reading and writing.

The caliph pointed to a bearded man sitting by a window, hunched over a pile of papers. The man was writing furiously.

"That is al-Khwarizmi," whispered the caliph. "He is a truly great mathematician. He has perfected the Indian way of writing numbers." The caliph pointed to numbers written on a board on the wall: *1, 2, 3, 4, 5, 6, 7, 8, 9, 10.* "We call these the Arabic numerals," he said.

"Arabic numerals?" said Jack.

"Yes," said the caliph.

Jack whispered to Annie, "We use the Arabic numerals, too. They must have come from that guy."

The caliph pointed to another man reading by the window. "He is al-Kindi. He is perhaps the most brilliant scientist and thinker in the world," whispered the caliph. "But he is very humble. He believes knowledge cannot belong to only one person or country. It belongs to all. The world grows wise only when wisdom is shared. I agree. And that is why I built this house."

"I agree, too," whispered Annie.

"Me too," said Jack.

"Scientists and scholars from many countries come here to read and study and share their knowledge," whispered the caliph. "We have thousands of books. They have all been copied by hand."

"By *hand*?" said Annie. "That's a *lot* of writing!"

"What kind of books?" asked Jack.

"Books of history, mathematics, geography, and medi-cine," said the caliph. "But we also have a very special book of fantasy and wonder."

The caliph took a large, thick book down from a shelf. He rested it on a table and turned the pages to show Jack and Annie. The book was filled with fancy writing and beautiful illustrations. There were pictures of Aladdin and Ali Baba, magic lamps and flying carpets.

"Oh, *Tales from the Arabian Nights*!" said Annie. "We know those stories."

"You do? Wonderful!" the caliph said with a smile. "It seems someone from our land has traveled to yours and shared our stories. Perhaps someone will soon bring stories from your land back to us. That is the great power of a book, no?"

"Yes," said Annie.

"And I hope your land will hear of this book, too, some-day," said the caliph. He held up the book of Aristotle's writings. "After I have read it, I will have it copied so I can share its wisdom with the world. Thank you for helping me."

"Sure," Jack said modestly. "That was our mission."

"I fear I must now return to my duties," said the caliph. "But please, stay in the library. Read until you must go to meet your family. And come back someday to visit me."

"We'll try," said Jack.

"Good-bye, Annie. Good-bye, Jack."

"Bye, Mamoon," Annie said.

The mighty caliph gave them a warm smile and a deep bow. Then he left Jack and Annie in his wondrous library.

Before the Moon Rises

Jack and Annie looked around the big room. The scholars and scientists were all deep into their reading.

"I can't believe Mamoon is the caliph," whispered Jack.

"*Remember that life is full of surprises,*" Annie repeated from Merlin's letter.

"Yeah, and *Return to the tree house before the moon rises,*" Jack finished.

"I almost forgot that part," said Annie.

"Me too," said Jack.

"Shh!" said one of the scholars and scientists.

"Sorry," said Annie.

Jack and Annie looked up at the open window. The sky was pink. The sun would be setting soon. "We have to get back to the tree house," Annie whispered, "before the moon rises."

"I know," said Jack, "but how?" He felt a moment of

panic. *The tree house is really far away*, he thought. *If we traveled on Beauty and Cutie, it would take a whole day and night to get there. And what about sandstorms? And bandits? Jack looked at Annie.*

She was smiling. *Magic*, she mouthed.

Jack caught his breath and nodded. They both looked around to see if any of the scholars or scientists were watching. They weren't.

Jack quietly slipped Teddy and Kathleen's book out of his bag. He and Annie turned their backs to the others and opened the book to the table of contents.

Annie pointed to *Turn into Ducks.*

Jack gave her a look.

Annie pointed to *Fly Through the Air.*

"Yes!" said Jack.

"Shh!" said a scholar.

Jack turned to the right page. He held up the book so they both could see.

Jack said the first line of the rhyme:

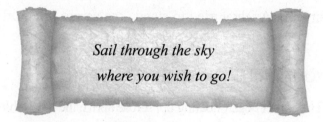

Sail through the sky
where you wish to go!

Annie said the second:

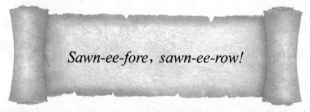

Sawn-ee-fore, sawn-ee-row!

"You must be quiet, or you will have to leave the library!" one of the scholars said grouchily.

"Don't worry, we're going," said Annie.

A wind blew through the tall open window, fluttering the pages of the *Arabian Nights* book. The scholars and scientists

grabbed their papers before they blew away.

The wind picked up a corner of the small carpet Jack and Annie were standing on. The carpet rippled. Jack and Annie fell forward. As they tried to stand，the carpet lifted off the floor.

"Oh!" cried all the scholars and scientists.

The carpet began floating up. It rose above the long tables. It rose above the shelves of books. Everyone jumped out of their chairs and scrambled out of the way，shouting，"Help!" — "Move!" — "Watch out!" — "Impossible!" — "What is happening?"

"Bye!" called Annie.

The carpet floated to the tall open window and glided out of the House of Wisdom.

Chilly air blew against Jack and Annie. Their head cloths flapped wildly as they clung to the end of the carpet and sailed through the sky.

"This is great!" cried Jack.

"*Really* great!" shouted Annie.

The carpet soared over the House of Wisdom, over the caliph riding back to his palace in his carriage, and over the camel stable.

The carpet zipped over the green dome with the horse on top. It flew over the courtyard, where the boys were still playing ball, over the third wall, and past the green field and the grand avenue.

The carpet flew over the second wall, the houses, the hospitals, and the hundred lions in the zoo. It flew over the first wall, the arched bridge, and the moat.

The carpet zoomed over the bazaar with the maze of stalls, the shoemakers, potters, and weavers. It sailed high over the road to Baghdad. Below, Jack and Annie saw the men driving donkey carts, the boys leading sheep, and the

women carrying pots.

The carpet flew faster and faster and faster—

over the river, the grazing fields,

and the dunes with the whistling sands,

over the red glowing desert

toward the setting sun

and the small oasis

in the middle of nowhere.

The magic carpet slid smoothly onto the scrubby grass,

near the small spring and the thorny shrubs, near the date

palms and the rope ladder.

The desert looked as if it were on fire with golden red

light. Jack felt giddy. "That—that was so fast!" he said.

"I can't believe we made it all the way here."

"No kidding," said Annie. "The magic must have

helped us stay on."

She and Jack tried to stand. They teetered and fell against each other.

"Steady," said Annie, giggling. "You okay?"

"Perfect," said Jack. He put his bag over his shoulder and staggered off the carpet. Then he and Annie headed over to the tallest date palm. Jack pulled the rope ladder from behind the trunk, and they climbed up.

When they got inside the tree house, Jack took out Merlin's letter. He glanced out the window one last time.

The sun was gone. The carpet looked small and ordinary in the shadows beneath the palm tree. The desert looked vast and silent and lonely. A thin crescent moon had appeared in the sky.

"Return to the tree house before the moon rises," said Jack.

"That was our last instruction from Merlin," said Annie.

"We're all done."

Jack looked down at Merlin's letter. He pointed at the words *Jack and Annie of Frog Creek*. "I wish we could go home!" he said.

The wind started to blow.

The tree house started to spin.

It spun faster and faster.

Then everything was still.

Absolutely still.

* * *

The Frog Creek woods were chilly in the afternoon air. Jack and Annie were dressed in their jeans and jackets again. Jack's shoulder bag was a backpack.

"Good trip," Jack said simply.

Annie nodded. "Really cool," she said.

"I guess we should get home," said Jack. "I have lots of

homework to finish."

"Leave the research book. But don't forget to take Teddy and Kathleen's rhyme book for safekeeping," said Annie.

Jack reached into his backpack. He pulled out the book on the golden age of Baghdad and placed it on the tree house floor. Then he threw his pack over his shoulder and climbed down the ladder. Annie followed. Together they walked through the early-spring woods.

"We passed Merlin's second test," said Annie. "We helped spread wisdom to the world.... That's a pretty big deal."

"Be humble," Jack reminded her.

"Well, I guess Teddy and Kathleen's book did the hard stuff for us," Annie said humbly.

"I miss them," said Jack.

"Me too," said Annie. "But I think they might have been with us in Baghdad."

"What do you mean?" said Jack.

"Remember that servant girl and boy who took us to the caliph?" said Annie. "They sort of came out of nowhere. And we never actually saw their faces, did we?"

"No...," said Jack. "You think?"

Annie shrugged. "Maybe."

Jack smiled and took a deep breath. "Maybe," he said softly.

"Two missions and five rhymes left," said Annie. "I hope Merlin sends for us again soon."

"But not *too* soon," said Jack. "I need to do my home-work first."

Annie laughed. "Math with Arabic numerals?" she said.

"Right," said Jack. "And maybe tomorrow we'll go to the library and see if they have any books of Aristotle's wis-dom."

"Good idea," said Annie.

A cool spring breeze rustled the trees, and Jack and Annie hurried toward home.

图书在版编目(CIP)数据

可怕的沙尘暴:英、汉/(美)奥斯本著;蓝葆春,蓝纯译.—武汉:湖北少年儿童出版社,2010.3

(神奇树屋:典藏版)

书名原文:Season of the Sandstorms

ISBN 978-7-5353-5017-6

Ⅰ.可… Ⅱ.①奥…②蓝…③蓝… Ⅲ.儿童文学—短篇小说—美国—现代—英、汉 Ⅳ.Ⅰ712.84

中国版本图书馆 CIP 数据核字(2010)第 040524 号

著作权合同登记号:图字:17-2006-050

神奇树屋典藏版 34——可怕的沙尘暴

原　　著:[美]玛丽·波·奥斯本
责任编辑:叶 珺　何 龙
整体设计:一壹图文

出 品 人:李 兵
出版发行:湖北少年儿童出版社
经　　销:新华书店湖北发行所
印　　刷:湖北恒泰印务有限公司

规　　格:880×1230　1/32　7.25 印张
印　　次:2010 年 4 月第 1 版　2016年8月第10次印刷
书　　号:ISBN 978-7-5353-5017-6
定　　价:16.00 元

业务电话:(027)87679179　87679199
http://www.hbcp.com.cn